The Ordeal of Anne Devlin

BOOKS BY ROBIN McKOWN

Fiction

JANINE

THE ORDEAL OF ANNE DEVLIN

Biography

SHE LIVED FOR SCIENCE
Irène Joliot-Curie

THE ORDEAL OF
ANNE DEVLIN

by

ROBIN McKOWN

LONDON
MACMILLAN & CO LTD
1964

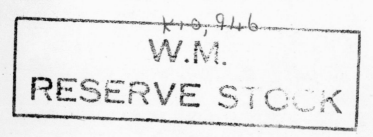

To

CARL AND SUE GLICK

Acknowledgments

The list of persons to whom I am indebted in my search for this book's background is a long one. I mention particularly Dr. Charles Dickson, author of *The Life of Michael Dwyer;* James G. Brennan and Piaras F. MacLochlainn of the Kilmainham Gaol Restoration Project; A. T. Lucas, Director of Dublin's National Museum; Mr. and Mrs. Michael Donnelly and Miss Kitty Moore, also of Dublin; Mr. and Mrs. Joe Dillon, Miss Nellie O'Brien and Master Thomas C. Herr, all of Aughrim (two miles from the Wicklow farm where Anne Devlin was born); Michael Lambert and the late Michael Redmond, both descendants of heroes of the Rebellion of '98; Walter Charles O'Byrne of Wicklow Town, and Mrs. Ena Bermingham of Barridarrig, Wicklow; Mrs. Joan Saunders of London; Miss Kathleen Cohalon, of the American Irish Historical Society in New York.

In addition, I should like to express my appreciation to R. J. Hayes, Director of the National Library of Ireland, for his courtesy in providing me with a microfilm of a manuscript on Anne Devlin by the Carmelite Brother, Luke Cullen (who interviewed her after her release from prison) and to R. B. McDowell of the National Library, an authority on nineteenth century Ireland.

RMcK

7

Author's Note

Anne Devlin's story, cloaked herein as fiction, is in essence true. The major characters are taken from life; in some cases physical descriptions come directly from police records of the time. None of the horrors Anne endured is exaggerated. No villain has been painted blacker than he was in real life, nor have the courageous and virtuous been given more glory than they merited.

RMcK

Contents

Part I

A COUNTRY GIRL

1

Episode in Inchicore

"You are a country girl, Anne Devlin, and ignorant like all Irish country people of the ways of the well-born. However, I have found you quick to learn, willing and cheerful. In letting you join our household staff, I give you an opportunity to improve yourself. I trust you will profit by it."

The words of Mrs. Heppenstall, the mistress of the house, echoed in Anne's ears as she stood in the butler's pantry, polishing glasses with a fine linen cloth. What lofty topics were the "well-born," seated in the dining room beyond, now discussing? All she could hear was the dark rumble of the voices of the men, the shrill laughter of the women, intermingled with the rattle of cutlery and crockery. She was barely past sixteen, slender in build and small in stature, with delicate pert features, deep blue eyes and a clear rosy complexion that revealed her country upbringing. A maid's cap was perched on her dark brown curls, and an apron was tied around the waist of her long cotton dress.

At her side, a wee boy no bigger than a midget—his name was Nicky—held the door open for the serving men as they went back and forth with their heaping platters.

"How can they be eating so much, Anne?" he asked, his eyes hungrily following the stream of roast turkeys, lobsters, beefsteaks, salmon, fricassee of rabbit, fillet of veal, and seemingly endless other dishes.

The first butler, a rakish-looking fellow for all his formal livery, stopped in the midst of uncorking the wine bottles, bending over to whisper: "It is because they are rich, my lad. Rich people all have *enormous* appetites. They gobble up land, houses, herds of cattle, fields of grain, money and even people without ever having indigestion at all. In this they bear startling resemblance to the English. Do they not, Anne Devlin?" He gave her a conspiratorial wink and passed on into the dining room, his basket of wines held high.

"Be he speaking the truth, Anne?" asked Nicky solemnly.

She knelt down beside him. " 'Tis a great banquet they are having tonight, Nicky, and there's no doubt on that. I watched the guests as they came in. Dukes and lords, I believe, and millionaires, with powered wigs and velvet jackets trimmed with lace and fine brocaded waistcoats. And their ladies in jewels and silk and satin, hoops so wide they must go sideways to pass through a door, and their hair piled at least a foot high, with a thousand pins to hold it there. The master's brother, Lieutenant Heppenstall of the Wicklow Yeomanry, who arrived today—he cannot say that his brother's wife does not receive the finest folk in Dublin."

Anne had been in the Heppenstall mansion, on Inchicore Road near Phoenix Park in Dublin's fashionable outskirts, for several weeks now, and still had not gotten over her wonder at so much grandeur. What stories she would have to tell when she got back to her parents' farm near Rathdrum in county Wicklow! She imagined the faces of her younger brothers and sisters as she described the stately red brick house, the carriages and handsome horses in the stable, the dozens of servants, the elegance of the visitors.

"I have a little brother at home almost as big as you," she told Nicky, her voice betraying a sudden nostalgia. "His name is Jimmy. He is round as a tub of butter and his cheeks are poppy-red."

The serving men returned with plates half emptied and set them down on the pantry table. Anne, as Cook had instructed her, scraped the leftovers into a row of wooden bowls. The bowls were for the beggars, who had been waiting hours in the back alley, for all the world as though their noses had caught the whiff of cooking as far away as the slums along Coombe Street.

The first butler reappeared, placing his hand on Nicky's thin shoulders. "Your duties are finished for the night, my lad. Get out to the kitchen. Cook has saved some choice morsels for your dinner." The boy darted out swift as a humming bird.

The man remained, watching Anne as she worked.

"And your duties, are they finished too, Timothy Campbell?" she demanded tartly. "Have you nothing better to do with yourself than to stand there staring?"

An attractive man, that first butler, all the women help agreed on that, with a store of sweet words that would melt a cake of ice, but Anne regarded him suspiciously. He was almost twice her age and she believed him to be a trifler.

"I was thinking," he said, his eyes still on her, "of a young girl, fresh and fragrant as a bouquet of spring flowers. I was thinking 'tis a pity to coop her up in a dark pantry hardly larger than a coffin."

"If it's of myself you are speaking, you waste your breath," Anne retorted. "You've no cause to pity me."

"Have I not?" he asked with the merest touch of sarcasm. "Are you still feeling indebted to Mrs. Heppenstall who, taking a fancy to you while visiting her sister, your father's landlady, persuaded your mother to let you come stay with her? Even now that you know she intended you, not for a companion, but for an unpaid servant?"

"Will you be quiet, Timothy Campbell?" Anne exploded. " 'Twas myself who asked for work to do, not being one to enjoy sitting with folded hands."

"Not that we're sorry to have you with us," he continued with that same ironic note. "You've won our hearts, from little Nicky to Cook, as crotchety a disbeliever as exists in all of Eire. But what about the lessons Mrs. Heppenstall promised—how to speak English as 'tis spoken in England, to write with a pleasing scroll, to embroider and to play the harpsichord?"

"She's had no time," Anne protested, flushing.

"Naturally not," he said with a shrug. " 'Tis far too much she has to do improving her social position. Come, Anne, are you still bewitched into believing that the Heppenstalls and their friends are far and away above the likes of you?"

"And are they not?" she cried. "They with their fine education, their travel to the Continent, their talk about matters of which I know nothing?"

"Are you not forgetting that you are Irish, Anne?" he asked, suddenly very serious, and turned and left her.

She looked after him in bewilderment. How could she forget for a moment that she was Irish? Was she not, on her mother's side, a descendant of the Irish chieftain, Feagh MacHugh O'Byrne? Was not an ancestor of the Devlins a confidential messenger of the famed Red Hugh O'Neill? Had not her family always opposed English tyranny? But the Heppenstalls and their guests were not English—true, some of them might be of English descent or birth, but they now claimed Ireland as their homeland. As her indignation against the first butler mounted, she scraped and stacked the plates with such vigor, the wonder was they were not smashed to fragments.

Patsy, a buxom young maid, rushed in to tell Anne to come with her—they were to serve coffee.

Timothy Campbell, wearing his impassive butler's face, was standing in the hallway entrance to the drawing room. Several serving men had gathered around the coffee samovar, giving the impression of being extremely busy, which they were not. It was the fashion of the time for a hostess to display as many servants as possible, even when they had nothing to do. It was also the custom to treat those servants as though they had neither eyes nor ears, except for commands. Anne and Patsy, passing around the coffee cups, might well have been puppets manipulated on a string.

The guests, having eaten and drunk to satiety, were in a state of lethargy. The ladies, seated on divans, their voluminous skirts spread wide around them, were languidly fanning themselves. One elderly gentleman was snoring peacefully in a corner. Mr. Heppenstall, stout and florid and nervously jovial, was trying to sustain conversation with the others but without success. Secretly, he was worried about the expenses of the evening; like many in his position he lived beyond his means. His brother, Lieutenant Heppenstall, in the red coat of an officer, stood by the mantel nursing a glass of brandy. He was the tallest man Anne had ever seen, well over seven feet, but with a small, round, mean face that went ill with his gigantic body.

A piper, hired for the occasion, was playing lilting tunes. No one seemed stirred by the music or gave evidence of even listening to it.

Without warning a shot rang out, followed by shouts and sounds of running footsteps. The elderly gentleman who had been snoring sat up with a start. The ladies stopped the movement of their fans. Anne felt a sick foreboding. Almost immediately there was a knocking at the front entrance. Timothy Campbell went to answer it and returned with a police officer.

"What is the meaning of this? What has happened?" blustered Mr. Heppenstall.

"I beg your Honor's pardon," the officer said. "We ran into a meeting of the Catholic Defenders in Phoenix Park, planning who knows what mischief. When they resisted arrest, we had to shoot—and one fell. The others came this way. We are checking the houses on the road to see if any tried to force entrance."

"They did not come here." Mr. Heppenstall, recovering his composure, gestured toward his aristocratic guests. "You can see for yourself we harbor no Defenders."

The police officer, with one look around, backed away hastily and apologetically. "Forgive me, your Honor."

Timothy escorted him to the door and did not return immediately.

Mr. Heppenstall, who was of English blood and made his living selling whisky to the Irish, paced back and forth across the floor. "We can blame the revolt of the American colonies for all this trouble," he declared pompously. "Up

until then we had the Papists well under control." "Papist"
was the word by which the English described Ireland's
large Catholic population. "The French Revolution added
fuel to the flame. These French and American ideas are
poison in the blood of the Papists."

The visit of the police had wiped away the apathy of the
gathering. The other gentlemen joined animatedly in the
discussion. One advocated revival and enforcement of the
penal laws which earlier in the century had deprived Catholics of such civil rights as education, voting, owning property and belonging to a profession. Another argued that a
few more reform measures would calm the unrest, but he
was immediately attacked by his fellows, while Mr. Heppenstall, forgetting his position as host, shouted, "Poppycock!"

One gentleman confided that already, in this year of
1797, the new United States of America was bogged down in
internal difficulties and that soon England would take over
again—a good lesson for the Papist heretics. Someone else
gloomily pointed out that it was no longer only Catholic
Defenders who were causing trouble; that the insurgent
United Irish Society had in fact the support of a number
of highly placed *Protestant* members.

Anne, still on duty, had listened unhappily to the sneers
against her own faith. At the mention of the United Irish
she froze. She had several cousins in county Wicklow who
belonged to this society, which made its appeal to all Irish
regardless of religion. They were sworn in under an oath
of secrecy. What could these gentlemen know about it?

At this point, the lieutenant, who had been devoting himself to his brandy, broke into such a prolonged giggle that
everyone turned to stare at him.

"The United Irish!" he repeated in his odd, high-pitched

voice. "We of the Irish Yeomanry know how to deal with them. I led a party the other day on a farmer at Gardenstown." His expression was childishly gleeful. "We told him that we knew he had weapons, and that if he did not show us where they were hidden, we would shoot him and his two sons on the spot. He tried to deny his guilt but finally led us to his garden where he had buried his musket and some ammunition. We forced him and his sons to dig them up, then shot all three anyway, and burned his house, crops and barns. We were very merciful. We let the women and children go free."

He looked around for applause, but his braggadocio manner had offended, and there were only a few polite murmurs. Anne noticed that Timothy Campbell had returned to his post. It seemed to her that he was unusually pale.

The lieutenant took another swig of brandy.

"There are some of them"—his "them" might have referred to insects—"who won't confess no matter what. Would you gentlemen and ladies like to know what I do then?" He giggled again and stretched up to his full height. "I take a rope." His gestures were realistic. "I tie it around the fellow's neck, then throw him over my shoulders—and there's an end to him. 'The Walking Gallows,' they call me. In town they've already made my epitaph." He chanted in an off-key voice:

> "Here lie the bones of Heppenstall—
> Judge, jury, gallows, rope and all."

There was an awkward silence. "My brother always was a prankster," Mr. Heppenstall said finally with a forced laugh. Mrs. Heppenstall, a large lady in a bright pink taffeta gown that went poorly with her sallow skin, wagged a playful finger: "I don't believe a word you say, Lieutenant. How naughty you are to make up such frightful tales." Everyone started to talk at once about the most inconsequential things.

Anne felt violently ill. Unnoticed by her mistress, she fled to the comforting darkness of the now deserted butler's pantry to sob out her revulsion. She had been there only a moment when Timothy Campbell entered.

"I am sorry, Anne Devlin," he said softly. "I am truly sorry. I wanted you to see for yourself the nature of the Anglo-Irish, those who give lip service to Ireland while supporting oppressive English policies, but I did not anticipate the lieutenant."

"He was speaking the truth, was he not?" she asked, wiping her eyes on a towel he handed her.

"Yes, he was."

"The beast!" she said. "The foul beast!"

"There are others like him."

"I suppose there are." She paused. "Why did you leave the room after the police officer?"

"Some friends of mine were in danger; I had to show them a safe hiding place." He added somberly, "That man who was shot in Phoenix Park—I knew him well."

"You are a Defender!" She looked at him with amazement.

"The Defenders are joining the United Irish now," he said. "Protestant or Catholic, their aim is the same: to break the chains that enslave Ireland."

"How I misjudged you!" she cried out. "And I thinking you were a frivolous man interested only in making pretty phrases to turn a woman's heart."

"You are not yet a woman, Anne Devlin," he said with a curious, twisted smile. "If I paid you more than common attention, 'twas that I saw you ill-suited to this house with its mask of greed and ambition and hypocrisy. You should go back to your native heath where you belong."

"I'll not go!" she said stubbornly. With an impulsiveness she could not have explained herself, she pleaded, "Let me stay and work with you, Timothy Campbell—for the cause of Ireland."

"I'll do no such thing," he told her firmly. "You don't know what you're asking."

The decision was taken from her hands the next morning when Mrs. Heppenstall came into the kitchen where Anne was helping Cook.

"Put away your apron, Anne. Your father is here to see you."

She found him in the vestibule, a tall, erect man with a strong black beard.

"Father, how glad I am to see you!" She threw her arms around his neck.

"I have come to take you home, Anne," he told her. "There be trouble brewing."

2

Beginning of a Rebellion

It was a dazzling morning, with the sweetness of hawthorne blossoms in the air, the larks singing overhead, and lovely Glenmalure Valley displaying its new spring greenery. With Little Arthur, her thirteen-year-old brother, Anne had been up in the boglands to gather a load of the neat squares of turf which their father had cut and stacked earlier in the season. The turf, which the English called peat, was their fuel, and sometimes their building material. Now they were returning home, their donkey and cart between them.

"Hurry up now, Miss Melinda." Anne patted the donkey's flanks. "Hurry up or we'll not be home for breakfast." She was wearing country dress—a scarlet petticoat reaching to her ankles, a tight-fitting jacket, laced in front, which left her arms bare, a kerchief pinned over her curls. "See how her ears twitch, Little Arthur? She understands every word."

Little Arthur, a sturdy youth with red hair and a quantity of freckles, was staring straight ahead, a scowl on his face.

"They arrested Mr. Finn, the blacksmith, yesterday," he said. "They accused him of making pikes for the United

Irish and they flogged him to make him confess. That was not right. Mr. Finn is a good man. He would not do harm to anyone."

Anne shuddered. Such stores had been all too frequent since her return from Dublin the year before. Since March Ireland had been under martial law. Their country was an armed camp, where some fifty thousand British Cavalry and Infantry, supported by at least thirty thousand Irish yeomen and militia, were stationed.

Brutes of the ilk of Lieutenant Heppenstall had invented varied and ingenious tortures for the United Irish, including "pitch-capping," covering the head of the victim with brown paper dipped in hot pitch. It almost seemed as though the authorities were purposely trying the patience of the people, to goad them to action.

"Why, there's the Master," said Little Arthur, pointing down the road.

Limping toward them was a gaunt, cadaverous figure in a shabby and shiny black frock coat and tall hat. Incongruously, his feet were bare. Over his shoulder he carried a dilapidated canvas bag.

"Good morrow, Anne! Good morrow, Little Arthur!" He raised his hat high.

They returned his greeting warmly, for they were both fond of him. For over a year, he had taught the children of the region secretly. On warm days he held his classes behind some hedge; on rainy days the children crowded into the shed which was his home. They paid him in potatoes and turf; he asked for nothing more. He was one of a heroic band of "hedge schoolmasters" who had taken over the schooling of the young when the penal laws forbade teaching to Catholic children, and were continuing this work now that the laws, in theory only, had been rescinded.

"You will wonder what I am doing at this early hour." He spoke in the exaggerated fashion of a man of learning. "This morning the militia broke into my tiny abode, rousing me from my slumbers with sound blows on the head, and ordering me to depart and be seen no more, else they would place me on a prison ship."

"The ruffians!" Anne cried out in distress. "Are you hurt badly, Master?"

" 'Tis nothing. Wounds of the body can be healed," he said. "The worst is that the ignoramuses burned my books—my Ovid, my Homer, my Vergil, copied out by myself in my own hand." Tears rolled down his sunken cheeks. "Ah, the Philistines, who could not see they were destroying a treasure more precious than the leprecaun's crock of gold."

"You are not going away, Master?" Little Arthur demanded anxiously.

"I must. It is not the first time I have had to seek a home among strangers. Continue to study my lad. Continue to improve your handwriting so you can copy the words of the great." He brandished his hat in the air. "Learn Greek! Learn Latin! Learn the poems of the great Celtic bards. Down with the barbarians! Long live Eire!" He bowed to them. "Farewell, my children." He saluted the little donkey. "Farewell, Miss Melinda. May we meet again when Ireland is free!"

He was off down the road, his ragged coattails fluttering behind him. Little Arthur looked after him with anguish.

"What will I do now?"

Anne knew what he was thinking. Learning was an obsession with her brother. The hours he spent with the Master, whose head was crammed with all manner of strange knowledge, meant more to him than anything. Now those hours were at an end, as was his youthful dream of becoming an educated man himself.

They were passing a small hamlet of mud houses occupied by cottiers, the desperately poor tenant farmers. None of their homes had chimneys. The smoke from the turf fires belched through the sod roofs, the cracks in the walls, the rag-stuffed windows, for all the world as though these wretched hovels were huffing and puffing with a life of their own. Dirty, near-naked children, were playing at the doorways. In front of one of them stood a woman with a bundle of nettles she had gathered from the fields. She was an emaciated woman, clad in rags, but there was a dignity about her that direst poverty could not efface. The two young people waved a greeting and passed on with their cart and donkey into a lane bounded by a moss-covered hedge.

"The poor things," murmured Anne, thinking of the cottiers' families. " 'Tis nettle soup they will be eating until the potato crop comes in. Or perhaps boiled charlock leaves, which turn the skin as yellow as does the fever."

"The Irish peasantry will starve as long as the rack rent system endures," announced Little Arthur, in a dictatorial manner that reflected the Master's teaching. "As long as large tracts of our land belong to Englishmen, who don't even live here, and who hire agents to let the land in small plots to the highest bidder, so that no man dare improve his property else he lose it."

"Thank goodness, we don't have to worry about that." Anne gave Miss Melinda a little prod. "Just a bit farther, my darling, and there's some fine sweet hay waiting for you."

The evil waters of misery, oppression and brutality swirled all around her and her family but had not touched them. They were in sight of the farm where Anne had lived since she was a child. With its thirty acres of tillage and pasture land, it was one of the best in the region. The industry and skill of Mr. Devlin were responsible for the good yield of the crops and the sleekness of the livestock. To the kindness of their landlady Mrs. Darby they owed the security that their land would not be taken away or their rent raised because of their improvements.

From the hillside, Anne looked down at their gleaming white thatched cottage, set among the crazy quilt of newly plowed fields. Daydreaming, she imagined how one day she would have such a cottage for her own, a husband as hard-working and good as her father, and a host of children, rosy and healthy. Her image of this future husband was nebulous. Though several young sons of farmers had cast appraising eyes on her, she had never been enmeshed in love's net.

"Psst! Anne! Little Arthur!"

They turned as two young men stepped from behind a bush. They were both tall and husky, with the same shade of auburn hair, clad in corduroy knee breeches, boots and brown jackets. Both carried muskets. They were Anne's first cousins—Big Art (so called to distinguish him from Little Arthur) and Patrick Devlin, sons of her father's brother. She had known them all her life; their sudden appearance startled her.

"What do ye mean popping out like that?" she scolded them.

"Ah, we've no time," said Big Art, without preliminaries. "Listen carefully now, the both of you. We wanted to say good-by to your father, but there's a chance we might be seen. The uprising is beginning. Today, all over Ireland, United Irishmen are headed for their assigned posts to drive out the English and their henchmen. The Good Lord knows we've had provocation enough."

Anne had suspected for some time that the uprising was inevitable, but she had not known how or when. Its reality was a staggering thing she could not at once accept. Her eyes filled with tears.

"Must you go?"

"Aye. There comes a time when a man must fight if he still wants to feel himself a man," Pat said gravely. "Michael Dwyer and Hugh Vesty Byrne"—he was referring to other cousins, sons of the sisters of Anne's mother—"have already gone on to Wexford. We're off to Newtonmountkennedy." This was a town a few miles distant. "Luck with us—and we'll take the barracks tonight."

"If I could only go with you!" Little Arthur's voice was wistful. He adored both his cousins, particularly Big Art, whose namesake and godson he was.

" 'Tis not a conflict for boys." Big Art put his arm around the youth's shoulders. "If we fail—it will be time for you. Mind, on your oath, not a word to anyone."

With a cheerful salute, they were off into the woodlands.

"May God's blessing be on you," Anne murmured after them.

It was May 26, 1798—a date that would live in Irish history.

3

The Two Refugees

"A sad loss!" said Bryan Devlin.

It was the day after Anne and her brother had seen Big Art and Pat off to the fighting. The family were gathered for supper. They sat on benches and stools around a long wooden table in the big clean kitchen, with its bog-oak rafters overhead, thick walls of wattle and daub, clay floor worn hard as rock. They were discussing the departure of the schoolmaster.

" 'Tis a shame!" commented Anne's mother, a frail, dark-haired woman with a strength of spirit that dominated her poor health. "He was a good man. A little strange, perhaps, but then who would not be with so many brains in one head?" She took the iron pot of steaming potatoes from the crane over the fire and set it on a stone slab before the hearth.

Anne's older sister Mary helped her transfer the potatoes into a large bowl. Mary was a gentle girl, so timid she rarely opened her mouth when strangers were present. Julie, a gamin of fourteen, with crinkly red-gold hair and a roguish look about her, filled the mugs with buttermilk and brought out a bowl of salt, in which they could dip their potatoes. A platter of salted herring, which their mother served from a barrel, completed the meal. It was simple but there was always plenty. The Devlins had never gone hungry and had never refused food to a beggar.

Anne sat between four-year old Jimmy and Nellie, who was five, making sure they ate properly.

"If there is no schoolmaster, we won't need to study, will we?" demanded Nellie. "We can play all day long."

"You cannot, my wee colleen," said Anne. "Even if I have to teach you myself, and it's little enough I know."

"For myself, I see no point in reading and writing," commented her other brother, John. At eleven, he was a dark, squarely built lad, large for his age. "What use is learning to a farmer?"

Anne was about to launch into a speech about the advantages of education for themselves, for all Irish patriots, when Tom Halpin, their landlady's gardener, appeared at their open door.

"Good evening, Bryan Devlin," he said, talking fast and breathlessly. "I come to warn you. There was fighting over at Newtonmountkennedy yesterday. Many patriots were killed and others were captured."

Anne and Little Arthur exchanged worried glances. Their father did not notice.

"A pity," he said, "For myself, I don't hold with fighting."

"The yeomanry are in the region, searching for men who escaped," continued the gardener. "I should tell you, Bryan Devlin, that your house is under special surveillance."

"And for what reason?" he asked. "We live a peaceful

life. We do our work. We stay out of other people's business."

"Everyone knows you are a peaceful man," Halpin said quickly, "and that your sons are too young for soldiers. But your nephews, Art and Pat Devlin, and the nephew of your wife, Hugh Vesty Byrne, the young brewer in Rathdrum. Did you know they have not been seen the last two days?"

"I did not." A look of annoyance crossed Bryan Devlin's face. "And how would you be knowing?"

"I heard in town." He looked over his shoulder as though fearing he might have been followed. "You know where my sympathies are, Bryan Devlin. If you need my help, you can count on me."

"Thank you kindly," he told the gardener, his face expressionless.

"Won't you stay for a mite of supper, Tom Halpin?" Mrs. Devlin asked him.

"No, I won't. You'll excuse me. 'Twas a chance I took to come here at all." He scooted away like a rabbit.

What an ugly little man, with his pointed nose, his red pock-marked face, his spindly legs! Anne quickly reproached herself for such uncharitable thoughts; Tom Halpin had always been a good neighbor.

Bryan Devlin rose, closed the door and lit the rush candles.

"Eat your supper," he said, seeing the frightened looks of the children. "If we mind our own business, we have nothing to fear."

Then they heard the hoofs of stamping horses, followed by a loud knock. Bryan Devlin rose and unlatched the door.

"What do you want?"

A group of Rathdrum Yeomanry, led by an officer, pushed their way in. They wore no uniforms; their insignia consisted of their red hatbands. Several were sons of tradesmen whom Anne knew by sight.

"You are Bryan Devlin?" the officer demanded. "The brother of Patrick Devlin?"

"I am."

"The uncle then of young Arthur and Patrick Devlin?"

"I am that."

"When did you see them last?"

"Perhaps a fortnight."

"They were seen at Crone Woods. We know they were at Newtonmountkennedy."

"I could not say as to that."

The officer conferred with his men. "We are going to search your house."

"Search then." Mr. Devlin resumed his seat at the table and continued his meal as though they were not there.

In a farmer's cottage there are no closets or other hiding places. They went into the bedroom of Anne's parents back of the fireplace. One of them climbed the ladder to the loft, stuck his bayonet through the straw where the boys slept. They looked into the third room of the cottage, opposite the fireplace, which Anne shared with Julie, Mary and Nellie.

"You are satisfied?" asked Bryan Devlin.

"I am sorry to have disturbed you," the officer said. He turned to Mrs. Devlin. "I will tell you, ma'am, it's making a great mistake they are. The ambitious scoundrels who started the United Irish have all been captured and have confessed their crimes."

Mrs. Devlin said nothing. Mary, her face flaming, had not looked up from the table. The younger children watched tensely.

"If you are through, you can be going." Bryan Devlin would not insult them, but he would not be cordial either.

Anne jumped up and held the door wide for them.

"The lackeys who betray their own!" she cried out when they had gone.

"Sit down and finish your supper, Anne," her mother told her placidly.

"I'm not hungry. I'll go feed the pig."

Outdoors, the dusk was sweet and heavy. A few stars glimmered faintly in the gray-blue sky. The farm was silent save for the cawing of a lonely crow and the grunts of their pig, louder, it seemed to her, than usual. She took a pan of potato mead and went down the sloping hill to his pen.

"Here, George!" she called, for they had named him, fairly or not, after the poor idiot king of England.

"Oink!" He moved over to her, a great lumbering, affectionate creature with pink ears and white bristly flanks. "Oink!"

"What is bothering you, my darling?" She had raised him from a piglet and loved him dearly.

"Oink!" He did not touch his food.

Something moved next to the turf lean-to that was George's home. Then two men rose from where they had been crouching.

"Be not afraid, lass," one of them said softly. "I am wounded as is my brother. We were told we might get shelter here for the night if we could get no farther." As they approached, she could see that both were young. One supported the other, and it was apparent they were in great pain.

"Who sent you?" she asked.

"One whom they called Big Art."

"I'll take you to my father."

"He'll not be turning us over to the authorities?" asked the one supporting his brother. "If you are not certain, lass, tell us and we'll be on our way. To be arrested now, 'tis death either by torture or execution."

Anne hesitated only briefly. "You can trust my father." Though he had paid scant attention to the talk of the United Irish, as plentiful as water in the well, she was confident he would not turn away anyone who needed help. She did not misjudge him.

"Well, my lads, it looks as though you have trouble," he said when Anne brought them to the door. "Come inside."

"My brother was shot in the leg at Newtonmountkennedy last night," one of them explained. "They got me in the shoulder. I am Terry Byrne and this is my brother John."

Bryan Devlin turned to the children, standing fascinated at the sight of the bloodstained visitors. "Get ye to bed now and forget what ye have heard." To his wife, he said, "Winifred, get them cleaned up and do what has to be done. Mary and Anne will help you. I'll hold the candles so you can see what you are doing."

Anne and her sister heated water, prepared bandages. In this moment of crisis. Mary forgot her shyness and worked quietly and efficiently. John Byrne's thigh had been grazed; the wound was not deep but painful. A bullet had lodged in Terry Byrne's shoulder.

"I'll have to get it out," Mrs. Devlin said, matter-of-factly. "It will hurt, my boy. Give him a drink of poteen from the jug, Bryan, to dull the pain." She made the patient stretch out on their table. "Cry out all you wish, but try not to move. Anne, hold his hand." With a small sharp knife she made the incision.

The youth clenched his teeth and did not utter a sound, but held onto Anne so tightly it hurt. His hand was large and brown, with the hardness of one who has plowed fields and flailed chaff from wheat since childhood, and the strength of it seemed to flow into her. Finally he fainted.

"Tis a good thing," commented Mrs. Devlin. "He can feel nothing." She probed quickly and deftly and at last held up the bullet she had extracted. "He'll be all right now. Some wet cloths and bandages, Anne."

The patient moaned, and there were drops of perspiration on his forehead. His face was tanned golden brown, and his hair was blond and wavy and thick. To Anne, he looked like a legendary Irish hero. He opened his eyes to see her bending over him, as she finished dressing his wound.

"I think I be in paradise," he whispered, "and that I be seeing an angel."

"He is delirious," Mrs. Devlin said quickly.

They put their two exhausted guests to bed in the loft with the boys.

Bryan Devlin sat down heavily before the smoldering turf fire.

"We'll have to think of something. If Tom Halpin was telling the truth, the yeomen will be back—and it will be no more safe for those two than for us."

"It would be dangerous," agreed his wife. "But they cannot get far until their wounds have a few days to heal."

"We cannot let them go to their sure capture," burst out Anne.

Her father silenced her with a look. "First thing in the morning, I'll go to Halpin. He offered to help and now he can do so. I'll ask him to keep the lads a spell in his house or barn. He'll not be suspect." The matter decided, he went off to bed.

"I wish Father would not send them away," blurted out Mary.

Anne looked at her in surprise. Her sister's pale cheeks were flushed with color and her eyes were shining.

"My daughters . . ." began Mrs. Devlin, and then stopped, shook her head as though the speech she had in mind seemed not worth the giving, and kissed them good night instead.

The wounded men slept late the next morning. When, with some difficulty, they climbed down from the loft, they claimed to be almost free of pain, but ravenous, confessing they had had nothing to eat but a handful of wheat kernels and nothing to drink but spring water for the past two days. A mound of cold potatoes vanished almost as fast as it appeared, as did mug after mug of milk.

Anne, Mary and their mother neglected their usual chores to wait on them. Julie and the little ones, Nellie and Jimmy, formed a mute but admiring semicircle around them. Little Arthur and John, with feigned indifference, sat down at the doorstep, but missed nothing that was said. To have wounded soldiers in the house—it was an adventure which did not happen every day.

In broad daylight, Terry Byrne was an even finer-looking man than Anne remembered from the night before—tall and blond and bronze. The thrill that had passed between them when he clutched her hand in his pain troubled her again. She turned away to hide her feelings.

His brother John was so different in appearance that it was hard to believe they were related. Of slender build, his hair was dark, his skin fair, his handsome face narrow and long. He was the more talkative.

"We come from near Castlekevin," he told them between mouthfuls. "Our father Owen Byrne is a farmer, known for his mighty strength. People call him Owen Kittagh, which means left-handed, and we are known as 'the sons of Kittagh.' Terry works the farm with him but I have never cared for farm life and am now a tailor. For all that, we are both our father's sons, and when he joined the United Irish we pledged our membership as well."

Mary, who was now mending his jacket, kept darting side glances at him as he spoke. Anne realized that he was the reason for her shining eyes, the rose in her cheeks, and no doubt for the pretty way she had arranged her hair that morning. But why not? Mary was nineteen, two years Anne's senior, and no less a woman for all she so seldom left her parents' roof.

Terry Byrne was displeased at his brother's outspokenness. "In these times it is well to guard one's tongue."

"But these are our friends. Have they not saved our lives?" John Byrne's expression was aggrieved.

" 'Tis all the more reason not to burden them with more than it is safe to know," Terry said.

Bryan Devlin walked in. He had left early to see Tom Halpin. At one look from him the children scattered. Anne built up the fire and Mrs. Devlin calmly cleared the table.

"How are you feeling, my lads?"

"In splendid form," said Terry. "Thanks to yourself and your wife and daughters."

"You will stay here today," he informed them. "At nightfall I will take you to a neighbor, where you can rest until you are well enough to travel. You will be safer there than here."

"You have already done too much."

"I do what has to be done." He stroked his beard thoughtfully. "You will, of course, speak to no one of where you have been."

"You can have our oath on that," John Byrne assured him quickly.

All that day he sat on the straw chair which they had purchased from a tinker, his bandaged leg stretched out on a stool. To entertain them he sang old ballads, and a few times Anne caught him talking in low tones to Mary at her spinning wheel. The radiance about her was like a light.

Terry Byrne, who had nothing wrong with his legs, followed Anne around as she did her chores, inside the house and out of it, his eyes on every move she made.

"My father and I live like bachelors," he said. "I had forgotten what a beautiful thing it is to see a woman doing woman's work."

With his good arm he insisted on carrying her pail of water from the well and helping her in other ways as best he could.

"You had better take a rest or your wound will be wide open again," she admonished him.

He smiled down on her. "You put temptation in my path. 'Twould suit me fine to be too ill to leave tonight."

Nonetheless he obeyed her to the extent of playing with the little ones and talking men-talk about guns and hunting and war and fishing with Little Arthur and John.

Came dusk and it was over. The men collected their blunderbusses from George's lean-to—for no man should be without his firearms, as they said. Mrs. Devlin, Anne and Mary walked with them to the pasture gate.

"And will you go home to your father now?" Anne asked Terry.

"To be arrested? Ah, no. When a man chooses a road like ours, there is no returning." So low the others could not hear, he added. "Never fear. I'll be back, Anne Devlin, and if it's on my own two feet I come, it will be for courting."

Something seemed to choke her and she could find no answer.

Nearby, she heard Mary laughing softly at something John Byrne was saying. At the gate, Mrs. Devlin ordered both men to do nothing beyond their strength, and, using her prerogative as a married woman old enough to be their mother, kissed them in farewell. Bryan Devlin joined them at that moment to guide them across the fields to Tom Halpin's. The women walked back to the cottage.

"My daughters," said Mrs. Devlin, "it is with love as with all growing things. A flower that blooms quickly, dies quickly. The hawthorne tree, growing slowly, lasts for a hundred years. This is a lesson which all women must learn."

4

First Love

Next morning, the yeomen burned down the farm of Patrick Devlin, the brother of Anne's father, because he would not, or could not, tell them where his sons were. Sick in bed with a fever, he would have perished in the flames had not one of the yeomen, more merciful than the rest, carried him out.

When news of the near tragedy reached the Devlins, Anne promptly rode over to Cronybyrne where her uncle lived, to offer their help. She found him lying on a heap of clean straw in the kitchen of a neighbor. Though he had lost all his worldly possessions, the grizzled old man was in excellent spirits. The womenfolk were doing all they could to make him comfortable. The men of the house were already planning to get other neighbors together to rebuild his cottage.

"Anne," he said, chuckling, "go back and tell your father that I am still on this earth only because the Devil did not want me and the Lord said I'd have to mend my ways before he'd have me." Surprisingly, he seemed to hold no resentment. She guessed that his sons would feel differently when they learned of it.

On her way home she stopped in Rathdrum, two miles from their farm, at the little house where her third missing cousin, Hugh Vesty Byrne, lived. He had a young wife, Rachel, and a baby, and she was worried lest they, too, should be pestered by the yeomen. But the house was closed and a neighbor informed her that Mrs. Byrne had taken her child and gone to her parents. Anne was certain Rachel would not have left had not her husband told her he would not return soon.

As she walked over to where she had tethered her bay mare, she met Magistrate Thomas King, a portly gentleman, much esteemed by her father. The two had known each other since childhood, and though Magistrate King was wealthy and a town official, he came often to their home to discuss agricultural matters with Bryan Devlin.

"Good day, Anne," he greeted her. "Tell your father if I have not been to see him lately, it is because of pressing duties." He added, "Our country has liberty fever. The best remedy is bloodletting."

Anne was not sure whether he meant what she thought he did; if so, she did not like it. For her father's sake, she made no comment.

Other villagers and country folk were being victimized as her uncle had been. Almost every morning when Anne looked across the fields she could see a cloud of smoke arising from the home of some unfortunate. There were cases of men being shot for no reason other than that they wore brown jackets, the only uniform of the patriot soldiers. Had the English, believing they had been too soft with the American colonies, decided on a policy of sheer terror for the Irish? There was plenty of evidence those days to this effect.

Their landlady Mrs. Darby, a fat, good-natured woman in rustling brown taffeta, drove up with her coachman and stormed into their house.

"Bryan Devlin, you're a good tenant and an honest man," she said, "and I do not blame you for your lawless nephews. I am having my son post a notice on your door, saying this is our property. Since he is a member of the Rathdrum Yeomanry, they won't dare to touch you."

"My thanks to you, Mrs. Darby," Mr. Devlin said morosely.

Still their landlady did not leave.

"It is folly—sheer folly—all of it," she went on. "Young men and older ones, leaving their farms and their work undone, streaming out to join an army that does not exist. Their leader is dead in prison. Do you know who he was? Lord Edward Fitzgerald, no less, from one of the finest houses in Ireland. A handsome, well-educated, wealthy young man, though they do say he was married to a French woman, which may have been the reason for his wild ideas."

"I know nothing of all that," Mr. Devlin said.

"My sister Mrs. Heppenstall wrote me all about it. A woman who knows everybody—everybody of importance—in Dublin." Mrs. Darby turned to Anne. "My sister sent you her greetings, my dear. She hopes you will make her another visit."

"My place it at home now," Anne said firmly.

The next day a man came and posted up the sign on their door, saying that their property belong to Robert Darby and was not to be molested. It annoyed Anne to see it there, like a banner proclaiming that their beautiful farm was not their own. Nor did her father have too much faith in it; that night he buried some kegs of oatmeal where they would be safe from marauders.

And still, in spite of Mrs. Darby's assurance that no army existed, sporadic fighting continued in their region. The United Irish scored a victory at Clough on June 4 and at Arklow on June 9, and news of them flooded the country with hope. In county Wexford, adjacent to Wicklow, the United Irish gathered more than ten thousand strong. They were joined by priests who had at first opposed the activities of the United Irish but changed their minds when they saw the appalling atrocities of the enemy.

"I saw Magistrate King in Rathdrum the other day," Bryan Devlin said after a trip to the market. "He told me that the British prime minister, William Pitt, has dismissed Lord Camden as Lord Lieutenant of Ireland, blaming him for pretending there were only Catholics in the uprising. The new Lord Lieutenant is Lord Cornwallis, the same whom the Americans defeated at Yorktown."

May he suffer the same fate here, breathed Anne.

Her wish was not granted. On June 22, two days after Cornwallis took office, the United Irish were defeated at Vinegar Hill in Wexford. Neither their warrior priests nor their ardent peasant farmers were a match for the well-trained, well-armed British troops. The rebels then attacked Hacketstown, fighting stubbornly for ten hours until they ran out of ammunition and had to surrender. A refugee reported that the fields where the fighting took place seemed painted with red lead.

On June 30, Lord Cornwallis offered amnesty to all the rebels who would lay down their arms. A few did so and were immediately slaughtered. Others took to the hills.

The yeomen paid another visit to the Devlin home. Because of the sign on the door, they were respectful.

"Are you the uncle of Michael Dwyer?" the officer asked Anne's father.

"Michael Dwyer is my nephew," interposed Mrs. Devlin quickly. "He is the son of my sister."

"I see." The yeoman paused. "Did you know that he was captain of the infamous outbreak at Vinegar Hill."

"I did not."

"I hope that if you hear where he is staying, you are good enough citizens to let us know. There is a reward involved."

In answer, Bryan Devlin walked over to the door and opened it. Anne had never seen him so angry.

This was their first inkling that Michael Dwyer was now the most sought rebel in county Wicklow. Within a few days his name was on everyone's tongue. Michael Dwyer and his band—estimated at from ten to a thousand—had refused an amnesty from Lord Cornwallis and had headed into the mountains. They alone in all of Wicklow—and with few exceptions in all of Ireland—refused to admit defeat.

Bold as brass, they descended one night upon the garrison at Rathdrum, bound and gagged the sentinels, seized a cache of ammunition from the very men who were supposed to be looking for them, leaving red faces behind. The gentry of the countryside were beside themselves with fright.

Mrs. Darby paid another visit. "Bryan Devlin, I have protected you and now I want you to do the same for me," she said. "I want you to tell Michael Dwyer and his men to stay clear of my lands."

"My wife's nephew is no bandit," Mr. Devlin said icily. "Go home in peace, Mrs. Darby. You have nothing to fear."

Despite all the excitement around them, life at the Devlin farm followed its normal course. Each older member of the family carried out his assigned chores, milking the cows, tending the sheep, working in the fields. Nellie and Jimmy grew tanned and healthy in the summer sun. The potato crop bloomed luxuriantly and the grain was tall and golden.

For all her numerous farm duties, Anne could not forget Terry Byrne's last words, "I'll be back, Anne Devlin, and if it's on my own two feet I come, it will be for courting." The memory of his brief stay was sweet in her heart, but painful too, as days and weeks passed without word of him.

Her mood of longing was sharpest toward dusk, that shadowy misty interlude between day and night when the soul of a young girl is tremulous with unformed desires, fraught with deep and reasonless despair, or flooded with a magic that makes the familiar earth a place of wonder.

Dusk was the time at which she was responsible for giving George, the pig, his evening meal, and George, whom she could trust never to reveal her secret, became her solitary confidant.

"Where do you suppose he be now, George?" she queried her pet one evening, as he came rubbing against her for his mead. "Do his thoughts ever turn to me or am I forgotten like a dream long past?" And then—impatiently, " 'Twas yourself presented him to me, remember? You should be able to tell me if he cares."

George only gave an indifferent "oink" and buried his snout in his mead, but then, just as on that memorable evening three months earlier, someone rose up behind his lean-to.

"Anne! Be not afraid. I have come as I promised."

Instinct, rather than recognition, told her that the words were spoken by the one whose name was written in her heart. Perversity, born of embarrassment, seized her and she turned sharply on him.

"What do you mean eavesdropping on me, Terry Byrne? 'Tis ashamed you should be."

He came closer. She saw that he was thinner and even more bronzed than on his first visit, and the expression in his eyes was both amused and tender.

"Sure I heard nothing but the sweet sound of your voice, Anne Devlin," he said. "For that I've traveled all day and all night through fields and forests."

"Why did you not present yourself at our door in the proper way?"

"I am an outlaw. To go to your house would bring danger to your family. Besides," he added, "it was yourself I wanted to see."

"You are speaking the truth?"

"Would I be here if it were not so?" He put his hands on her shoulders. "Aye, you are as I remember you, full of spirit as a colt but with a heart as warm as any I have ever seen. Anne Devlin, I've fought with the patriot army at Vinegar Hill and lived a soldier's life with its fare of blood and death, and through it all I've been half daft missing you and yearning for you."

He let his hand stroke her hair. "You don't have to speak if you've not a mind to. I must be off quickly in any case. Listen now. At the present I'm working as a farm helper over yonder where no one knows me, but when the trouble is over I'll return to my father's farm, which will one day be mine. Anne, there's only you with whom I want to share my life. . . ."

As he spoke there was a whirring in her head like the wings of a troop of fairyfolk. To love and to know oneself beloved, it was an ecstasy almost beyond bearing, one not forbidden to simple people like herself.

"Ah, Terry!" she murmured, and felt his arms tighten around her."

Like a warning, her mother's words came back to her: "It is with love as with all growing things. A flower that blooms quickly, dies quickly." How wrong her mother was! She felt certain that her love, born almost overnight, would endure forever.

"We know each other such a small time." She spoke only to convince herself. "How can we be sure?"

He gave her a hurt look. "But I am sure. I'm twenty-six and I've waited long enough to know what I want and no mistake. Even to seeing my younger brother John married before me. . . ."

She caught her breath. "Your brother John is a married man?"

"He is. Did we not mention it?"

"You did not. Why, then, was he making sweet talk with my sister Mary?"

Terry shrugged. "It is his way with all women."

"My sister is not 'all women.' She is gently reared and not used to the trickery of men."

"He meant no harm."

"And is it also your way to make sweet talk with women?"

"It is not."

"Why should I think you different from your brother?" she demanded.

"If you don't know why, then you are filled full with nonsense," he said with an injured air.

"Filled with nonsense, am I?" She couldn't keep her voice from rising. " 'Tis a good thing I found out now your true feeling."

They both stood apart glaring at each other.

"Anne! What takes you so long? Come back at once." Her father's stern call interrupted them.

"Yes, Father!" she called back. And to Terry, "I must go."

"I know," he said stonily.

"Good-by, Terry Byrne."

"Good-by, Anne Devlin."

They might have been two strangers. He turned and started off. She watched him disappear into the darkness. There is an end to that, she told herself sadly. Suddenly, as if by no volition of her own, she was running after him.

"Terry!"

"What is it, Anne?"

Instead of answering, she reached up and kissed him, gently and fondly, much as her mother had done the other time he left.

In later years there were many things in her life which she might have wished changed, but she never regretted the kiss she gave Terry Byrne on that night.

5

The Outlaw Cousins

In the few weeks since Anne's cousin, Michael Dwyer, had been in hiding, his name had become a legend. The English had sent in reinforcements. The Yeomanry had conducted a systematic search. They often found out where Dwyer and his men had been, but never where they were.

The family of Michael Dwyer lived at Eadstown, the other side of the mountains, some fifteen miles away. It had been some time since the Devlins had news of them when, one fine crisp morning in September, Kathy Dwyer, Michael's oldest sister, paid them a visit. A tall husky young woman with dark hair and olive skin, she came riding a dapple-gray pony, bringing greetings from her mother, the sister of Anne's mother.

The Devlins plied her with questions. Yes, they were all well, she said. The yeomen and the militia descended on them regularly, questioning them and searching their premises again and again, but so far that had been all. None of them had been arrested, nor had their home been burned, as had so many others. Perhaps they were afraid of the vengeance of Michael Dwyer, should they try such tactics. The matter-of-fact manner in which Kathy accepted their constant danger impressed Anne deeply.

"How dreadful it must be for you not to know where Michael is," she commented later in the morning, while she and Kathy, arm in arm, were making a tour of the farm.

"But I do know where he is," Kathy informed her. "Michael and your other cousins as well."

"You do? How I would love to see them!" Anne exclaimed wistfully.

"They want to see you too, Anne dear," Kathy said. "That is one reason why I am here. I will ask Aunt Winny and Uncle Bryan to let you come home with me and spend the night. Then I will take you to visit them. Would you like that?"

"It would give me more pleasure than anything," Anne assured her.

Rather to her surprise, her parents consented to the trip. "The change will do you good," her mother said. "You have been looking pale." "Be careful and take no chances," her father warned her. "Come back early enough to do your chores."

Only her sister Mary seemed to guess the real purpose of the voyage. "Should you see any of our cousins—or friends— tell them I pray for them regularly." Mary had become more remote and dreamy than ever since the night the Byrne brothers spent on the farm. Anne had never had the courage to tell her that John Byrne was a married man.

She and Kathy set off shortly after their midday meal, Anne riding her bay mare and wearing her sturdiest clothes. It was exhilarating to gallop in the shadow of the great Lugnaquilla, the highest peak in Wicklow, along the narrow road which skirted the green hills, stained with purple heather. Kathy was as good a horsewoman as Anne. As their pace slackened, Kathy pulled up and rode at her side.

"What do you know about the United Irish, Anne?"

"Why, not too much," Anne admitted, "excepting that they want all Irish to join together to fight for freedom."

"They were founded in Belfast in 1791," said Kathy, "by two young men: Theobald Wolfe Tone, the son of a humble coachmaker, and an army officer named Thomas Russell. With their so different backgrounds, they had in common a love of Ireland. Another of their leaders was Thomas Addis Emmet, a brilliant lawyer; he is the son of the state physician of Dublin. Russell, Emmet and most of the society's leaders are in prison now. There was an informer in their midst. These are things one should know."

"And Lord Edward Fitzgerald?" asked Anne, remembering what Mrs. Darby had said.

"A brave and gallant man. After the arrest of the others, he became the military leader. Possibly the same informer betrayed him. He died in prison of his wounds just a few days before our uprising. Even had we known, I think nothing would have changed. How could one cry 'patience' to a storm erupting?"

"And is all lost now? Is here no hope?"

"There is. Wolfe Tone is in exile in France, seeking French aid. If the French send an expedition, and they might well do so, the Irish will certainly rise to join them. That is what Michael Dwyer is waiting for. That is what he is hoping for."

"How do you know so much about the United Irish, Kathy?" Anne asked.

"From Michael Dwyer. Who else? Do you think he would

not be finding out everything possible about it, seeing that it has become his life?"

By the time the sun was setting, they had reached Knockgorragh, on the border of the Vale of Imaal, a strange and lovely valley, fragrant with pines and full of secret springs and dells. Kathy rode up to a low white thatched cottage, almost hidden in a cluster of willow trees, and drew in her reins.

"Be anyone at home?" he called out.

A big and cheerful farmer came out and greeted them. Kathy introduced him as John Cullen. They dismounted and went inside, where his wife, a thin, energetic woman, made them sit down by the fire and served them buttermilk and oat cakes. After a whispered consultation with Kathy, the farmer left. He was back shortly.

"All is set," he said, nodding at Kathy.

She rose. "We will leave our horses with you, John Cullen. Come, Anne."

They had walked about a quarter of a mile down a narrow lane, when Kathy stopped and let out a whistle. At once Anne heard footsteps behind them.

"It's Michael," whispered Kathy.

When they reached a wooded glen, far from any human habitation, he caught up with them.

"Well, now, my little cousin, Anne Devlin," he said, grinning. "Be you not frightened at the company of outlaws?"

"When I shall be frightened by you, Michael Dwyer, the river Slaney will be running gold," she retorted.

She remembered him as a good-natured, obliging youth, always ready for a romp with his own younger brothers and sisters, and the Devlin children. At twenty-six, he was a tall, thick set man, dark like his sister, with coal-black hair, wide-set eyes, large mouth and a slightly upturned nose. Except for his musket and his high mountain boots, he might have been any farmer's son home from haying.

"Kathy and I are taking you to one of my country seats," he told her, his eyes twinkling. "Your cousins, Hugh Vesty, Pat and Big Art are there."

The moon came up, casting an eerie glow over the landscape. He led them up a steep hillside, across the marshy bogland, through a long stretch of bracken, a large fernlike bush too dense for the passage of a horse, but offering perfect protection for a man in hiding.

"I see why they have such a time catching up with you, Michael Dwyer," Anne panted after him.

"Oh, we have not yet started, Anne, my darling," he said, giving her a helping hand.

On they went, up and down cliffs, skirting precipices, wading through more marshes, with Michael Dwyer making jokes and telling stories, as though all this was no more than a Sunday stroll. At last they came to a large rock where he stopped.

"This is it, my country seat," he announced mysteriously.

Anne looked around, expecting to see some sign of human habitation, but there was none. Then Michael turned his back to the rock and struck it with his heel, at the same time shouting some strange words. Before her eyes, she saw a large bush of heather rise up in the air. Where it had been was the entrance to a tunnel, reflecting the faint gleam of a candle.

Three men scrambled out, one at a time. They were Art and Pat Devlin and her other cousin, Hugh Vesty Byrne, a sandy-haired young man of twenty-two. They looked healthy and cheerful, and only their worn and torn clothes showed how long they had been without a woman to wash and mend for them. Gathering around Anne, they praised her for having made the arduous journey to see them.

"And I worrying my heart out about you, not knowing what terrible thing might have befallen you," she said, half laughing, half sobbing. "I should have known you could take care of yourselves."

They demanded news of their families and friends, and she told Big Art and Pat that their father was now settled in his new cottage and fully recovered from his fever.

To her surprise, they scowled.

"We know who burnt his cottage now, and who were willing to let him burn with it," said Big Art grimly. "The ringleaders were George Manning, the coroner, and his sons. They are to be punished for their dastardly act."

"Must it be you who does it?" cried Anne, thinking of the danger to them.

"Who would do it if we did not?" broke in Michael Dwyer, his face suddenly stern. "Anne, against such as Manning, we are waging implacable war."

She had no answer. In their lovely land, justice for the victims of military outrages was nonexistent.

As Michael stood, unyielding as a granite statue, Kathy seized his arm. "Come on, Michael. Show Anne though your 'country seat.' "

"Of course," he said, his face relaxing into smiles. "Follow me."

He led the way down the tunnel which the heather had concealed, with Anne and the others scrambling after him. Anne found herself in a large underground room, lined with moss. Arms and equipment were arranged along the walls, orderly as in an army barracks. About a dozen men were playing cards by the light of the candles, as merrily as if they had not a single care.

Michael Dwyer took Anne around and presented all of them to his "little cousin." He stopped before a dark, homely man of about thirty.

"This is Martin Burke, my second in command, Anne. Tonight we are celebrating his escape from the Baltinglass guardhouse. With his arm fastened to his side by an iron band, he slipped away from his captors, crossed the river, hid in a ruined abbey, found a smith to break the lock of his irons, then rejoined us here."

She heard many other tales that night of close brushes with death or capture, all told with high relish, as though danger was the food that nourished them.

When Kathy announced it was time to leave, Arthur, Pat and Hugh Vesty joined Michael Dwyer to escort them back over the precarious way they had come. The moon had gone down and their only light was that of the stars.

"Now that you have seen how we live, Anne," said Michael, who held her arm to keep her from stumbling, "do you not think it is a fine free life?"

"And when winter comes? What will you do then?" she demanded.

"Never fear. We have other shelters. The farmers around here are with us. We can hold out as long as need be."

"And how long will that be?"

"Not I nor any man living can tell you that," he said solemnly. "Of one thing I am sure. The torch of liberty is flaming. No matter how many fall, there will always be someone to carry it until Ireland is free again."

As if embarrassed to find himself uttering such noble phrases, he changed the subject. "Look," he said, picking up a sprig of yellow gorse. "Is this not a lovely thing? They say that sweethearts stop kissing when the gorse stops blooming, and since the gorse blooms all the year round, there is no end to the kisses of sweethearts. . . ."

"Is Michael telling you about his sweetheart?" called Kathy, a few steps behind them.

"No, he isn't," said Anne. "I did not know he had one."

"A fine handsome girl, Mary Doyle," Kathy continued, catching up with them. "I shall be proud to have her as a sister-in-law."

"Congratulations, Michael!" She added, teasingly, "However did you find time for courting?"

"You have a long tongue, sister of mine," Michael growled. But he did not seem displeased.

"Why anyone would want to marry a man who never rests his head two nights running in the same place is more than I can say," Kathy commented dryly. "But for tastes there's no accounting."

The others joined in the banter. There was no more serious talk that night.

When Anne rode home a few hours later, Little Arthur ran down to meet her. "The yeomen were here again last night. They questioned us about our cousins, but we could tell them nothing."

She had wanted to tell her family about her nocturnal adventure. Now she knew it was safer for them to keep it to herself.

The crimes against the people had diminished these last weeks, under instructions from Lord Cornwallis it was said, but they did not cease. On October 1, a yeoman, Hugh Wolloghan, shot and killed a feeble old man named Dogherty for no reason but the sport of it. There were witnesses, and the Dogherty family brought charges against the assassin. At the trial, Lieutenant William Tomlinson, Wolloghan's superior in rank, testified to the innocence of the prisoner. He was acquitted, departing at once for Dublin to escape the wrath of his neighbors, which was turned on Tomlinson, now considered equally guilty.

A few days after this mockery of a trial, Tom Halpin, the gardener, came rushing over to the Devlin farm with the news that Lieutenant Tomlinson's house had been burned to ashes, as had that of the coroner, George Manning. Michael Dwyer and some thirty of his men had been seen in the neighborhood.

"General Eustace has been brought in from Arklow with a detachment of five hundred soldiers," Halpin continued. "Michael Dwyer has gone too far this time. He is sure to be caught." To Anne, his ugly face seemed twisted with pleasure.

The next morning at dawn, a contingent of English soldiers came banging on their door. Only Anne and her parents were up.

"We have come to arrest you, Bryan Devlin," the captain announced.

"On what charge?" he demanded.

"On the charge of aiding and abetting the wanted criminal Michael Dwyer."

"It is false. Michael Dwyer has neither asked nor received my help."

"We are not here to argue," the captain said. "You are to come with us."

"You have no right!" cried Anne. "You have no right to take an innocent man."

"Be silent, Anne," her father told her. "Words are not to

be wasted." He put on his homespun jacket, gave his wife a few words of advice about farm chores, embraced them both and turned to the captain. "I am ready."

Mother and daughter stood in the doorway looking after him. The sight of her proud bearded father being pushed along like a common thief cut Anne like a knife.

"They have no right," she repeated numbly. "Mother, what are we to do?"

"Have no fear," her mother said. "God will see that justice is done." But even as she uttered consoling words, she was racked with sobs.

6

A Home Without a Father

Bryan Devlin was taken to the gaol in Wicklow Town, a fishing village on the coast about fifteen miles away. As soon as they learned his whereabouts, Mrs. Devlin sent Anne to see him with a basket of freshly baked oat cakes and some clean linens.

It was a clear, crisp morning, the trees lining the road were decked in the splendor of their autumn hues. Anne's bay mare winnied, tossed her head high, fairly dancing with delight at this unexpected excursion. Anne would have enjoyed herself equally had not the earth's loveliness seemed a mockery as long as some people had the power to deprive their fellow men of the sight of it.

Wicklow goal was a gloomy fortress at the far end of town. The guard at the gate, after making her wait outside interminably, turned her over to a turnkey, who took her down a hall lined with cells. Behind the iron bars the prisoners paced like animals in a zoo. Several called her name. They were friends and neighbors.

She saw her father before he saw her. He was standing

motionless in the center of his cell. With his gaunt face, his black beard and his dark, deep-set eyes, he resembled some holy martyr of biblical times.

The turnkey twisted the key in the lock. "Ye have a visitor, Bryan Devlin!" he called as the cell door swung open.

Her father's features softened as he recognized her. " 'Tis good to see you, lass."

Unable to restrain her emotion, she threw her arms around him, told him how much they missed him, gave him the kisses and messages of affection with which the rest of the family had entrusted her. He released himself and bade her sit down on a low stool.

"Listen carefully, daughter. To tear a farmer from his farming is to drive him half out of his senses. I cannot rest until you know what has to be done." He launched into a torrent of instructions and admonitions about planting and sowing, threshing the hay, treating cattle swollen from too much fresh clover, about the ewes to be brought down from the highlands and the cow which was soon to calve.

"Father, there's no need," Anne pleaded finally, her head swimming. "You will soon be home with us, able to run the farm to your own liking. How could it be otherwise, since you have done nothing and nothing can be proved against you?"

He shook his head. "I am a peaceful man and have always minded my own affairs. Once I thought that was enough. Now I am beginning to ask myself questions."

On her way out she was stopped by the head gaoler, a stout red-faced man named Charles Carr.

"A fine man, your father," he said. "I am glad I could keep him with us instead of sending him off to a prison ship with the others for whom there was no room here. Horrible places, those prison ships!" His gaze took in her neat dark blue cloak and hood. "A prosperous man, your father, able to dress his daughters well. You will not want him to live on common prison fare."

It was not difficult to grasp his meaning. "You arrest him, keep him from doing his proper work, and expect him to provide his own food as well?" she asked.

"What can I do?" He threw out his hands in a gesture of helplessness. "It is a rule. We can feed only those who would otherwise starve."

She did not need to ask into whose pocket went the money saved by such a "rule." From then on, she rode twice a week to Wicklow Town, rain or shine, sleet or snow, to carry provisions for her father. Her mother sent her rather than Mary, who was as afraid of horses as she was of people. Occasionally Little Arthur or Julie went with her, but mostly she was alone.

The misfortune that had struck her own family made Anne more sensitive to the troubles of others. As often as she could, she made the trip around the mountains to the Dwyer farm, where her aunt and uncle and Michael Dwyer's six younger brothers and sisters lived. With Kathy, who had taken her to Imaal, and Mary, the next youngest, she struck up a special friendship. Both these young women were older than she, but all three had in common a spirit of daring rare in women.

Sometimes they were joined by Kathy's new sister-in-law, the former Mary Doyle, a tall, handsome, dark-haired woman who had married Michael Dwyer the very night of the burning of the Manning and Tomlinson houses. Immediately after the ceremony he and his men had taken to the hills.

She saw her husband frequently, but how and where those meetings were arranged she did not tell.

Contrary to Tom Halpin's predictions, the combined forces of the Rathdrum Yeomanry and the five hundred soldiers of General Eustace of Arklow found no trace of the outlaws. General Eustace's prestige suffered from this failure. "He has lost a step in his elevation," the peasantry said, but more troops were sent in.

On the snowy night of February 15, 1799, a British Highland regiment surrounded a cluster of cottages in Derrynamuck, on the edge of the Vale of Imaal. An informer had reported that Dwyer and some of his men had taken shelter there. Eleven were captured, executed at Baltinglass the next day, and buried in the churchyard at Kilranelagh.

That Michael Dwyer escaped was due to the courage of his comrade Sam McAllister. Soldiers called to them to come out of the cottage where they had taken refuge, but they refused. There was shooting on both sides. The soldiers set fire to the thatched roof and smoke filled the cottage. It looked as though they had the choice of dying in the flames or surrendering. McAllister was hit by a ball which fractured his right arm.

"I am done," he told Michael Dwyer, "but you must take my advice. Load your blunderbuss and give it to me; go on your hands and feet. I will open the door and stand upright and discharge the blunderbuss. They will fire at me and you may be off before they load again."

McAllister was killed instantly, but Michael had time to take off into the woods, eluding his pursuers.

"Poor Sam McAllister," sighed Kathy Dwyer, who gave Anne the details of this story. "His body has been left at Leitrim, covered only with hay. Our men don't dare try to

bury him; they would be shot. Mary and I plan to take him
to the Kilranelagh churchyard, so he can rest in death with
his comrades in life. Will you go with us?"

Not without some inner qualms, Anne assented. Never to
be forgotten was that dark and windy night when the three
daughters of farmers drove across the valley in an open
wagon holding the coffin with the remains of the brave Sam
McAllister. There were two yeomen on guard at the churchyard when they arrived. Ignoring them, the young women
lowered the coffin into the open grave prepared in advance,
covered it with earth and then knelt to pray. The yeomen
watched curiously but did not try to stop them.

The whole countryside was thrilled that Sam McAllister
had a proper burial. Many young women claimed to be
heartbroken because they were not included in the eerie
adventure. Anne and the Dwyer sisters proposed they all
collect ribbons and silks and make funeral garlands, a sug-
gestion that met with great enthusiasm. Dressed in white,
they marched in a long procession to the churchyard at
Kilranelagh, where they laid their garlands on the graves
of their heroes and offered up prayers to all those who had
given their lives in the cause of liberty. After this, the authorities could not doubt that the sympathies of the people
were with those they called "outlaws."

Soon after this event, Anne arrived at Wicklow goal to
find her father in the exercise yard with the other prisoners.
One of them was a giant of a man with a heavy red beard
streaked with gray. A chain was attached to his leg at the
end of which was a massive iron bolt. This he lifted as
though it were made of straw, but when the others tried to
do the same they would hardly budge it.

"Who is that?" she asked her father.

He called the giant over. "Kittagh," he said, "this is my daughter Anne."

The man beamed on her. "A darling lass, Devlin," he said. "Aye, if we were free I would be smoking a pipe on your doorstep, conniving with ye to make her the bride of my eldest son."

"Owen Kittagh Byrne," explained Bryan Devlin, "is the father of those two lads you and your mother doctored some-time back."

Anne felt herself flushing. "And how are your sons, Mr. Kittagh?" she managed to ask.

"As far as I know they are safe, God bless them." His face contorted with sudden pain. "Aye, if by giving me own life I could keep them that way!"

When Anne came the next time, Owen Kittagh Byrne was no longer there.

"He asked to go to his death as a United Irishman, wear-ing a green stock at his neck," her father told her. "The request was denied. A pity!"

As the months passed, Byran Devlin had become increas-ingly concerned with the problems and sufferings of his fellow prisoners. He still gave Anne spasmodic advice about the farm, but it was clear that for him the small world of the gaol now obscured the larger one outside.

"Hugh Vesty is here," he confided one day in late spring. "He was captured on a mission to Dublin. A disgrace he should be behind bars while that scoundrel Gaoler Carr walks free. There was never a more generous lad. Persuade the turnkey to let you see him, Anne. As a known comrade of Michael Dwyer, there is little doubt what sentence he will receive."

A bribe to the turnkey got her into her cousin's cell. He

was in almost as good spirits as on that night at Imaal. "Don't look so sorrowful, Anne," he told her. "If I die, it will be with my head held high. Can a man ask for more?"

But he did not die. When next she came his cell was empty. With another condemned prisoner, he had escaped by means of a pole which some workmen had left near the gaol wall. Soon after, he rejoined Michael Dwyer.

Her father, usually so grave, chuckled at the news. "The lad outwitted them. Wherever you find anyone named Byrne, you find a man worthy of Ireland."

It was truly amazing how many Byrnes in the region were rebels. That September Billy Byrne of Ballymanus, a young man who was extremely popular with the women because of his charm and good looks, was executed on perjured testimony. The whole countryside was outraged. One of the witnesses against him was a simple-minded girl named Bridget Dolan, nicknamed "Croppy Biddy" because she wore her hair cropped short. Anne met her on the road to Wicklow Town, wearing a new red cloak and leather shoes. Previously she had always seen her barefoot and in a shabby dirty gown.

"What fine new clothes, Biddy!"

The girl pranced coquettishly before her. "Aren't they now? I got them because I said that Billy Byrne was a murderer."

"But Biddy, that was a lie and you know it. You helped to send Billy to his death."

"What do I care about that?" the girl demanded sulkily. "He never paid attention to me when he was alive. For myself, he is better off dead."

The government brought in more soldiers, using them to construct a military road stretching from Dublin through

E

Glendalough and Larach into the heart of the Wicklow Mountains. In this way, they hoped to expedite their search for Michael Dwyer—the first time in history a road was built to find one man. They failed in this, but through informers they arrested John and Terry Byrne. Anne learned of the arrest but could not find out where they were being kept.

One gray September day of 1800, she was at the market in Rathdrum with her mother and Little Arthur. A crowd was gathered at the public square. They stopped to see what was happening.

"They have hanged John Murphy," an old woman told them. "They tried to get him to kneel on his own coffin, but he refused and jumped up and down on it and broke the lid. The soldiers were furious."

Anne did not know John Murphy, but her eyes filled with tears for him.

The soldiers brought forth another prisoner, a tall young man with red gold hair. His hands were tied behind his back, but he held himself straight and proud as he took his place in the shadow of the gallows.

"Terry Byrne!" Anne pushed forward, unheeding the grumblings of those she shoved aside, until she reached the edge of the green.

What she intended to do, she could not have said. That she loved Terry Byrne and wanted one day to marry him, she was thoroughly convinced, but, since Fate had not permitted her to become accustomed to his presence, she had not really been unhappy without him. Her memory of their few brief and poignant secret meetings was rather like a cool well, deep within her, where she could retreat from time to time to drink a blissful potion that effaced the hardships of her daily life. She could not now stand still and witness his destruction.

"They cannot do this monstrous act!" She started to run forward.

"It's no use, lass," said a stranger nearby. "We are not yet strong enough."

A contingent of soldiers stepped forward, barring her way with their muskets. Terry Byrne, made aware of the disturbance, turned his head and saw her standing there. His face became serene, as though his last wish on earth had been granted, and he smiled at her.

She felt her mother's hand on her arm. "Come away, Anne. Little Arthur will take you home. I will be along presently." When she still stood rigid, her mother added, "Obey me now."

Dumb with pain and horror, she allowed Little Arthur to lead her way.

Hours later their mother drove their wagon into the farmyard. She was pale but there was an air about her of one who had done what must be done. The children gathered around her, demanding what had kept her so long. She patted them absent-mindedly, making no reply. Only after the others were asleep did she take Anne aside.

"I waited till it was over, Anne, and then I went to the sheriff and demanded his body, for he had no family to claim him and I could not leave him to the mercy of those ruffians. An old man helped me put him in the wagon and I went and found the priest. He is buried in the churchyard and prayers have been said over him. It was the least we could do for him."

In the midst of her own fearful sorrow, Anne found it possible to wonder at her frail mother's courage. "You are putting yourself in danger, Mother," she said dully. "They will not forget what you have done."

"So be it." Her mother sighed. "He was a good lad. I learned he was charged with murdering a certain John Mason at Ballynultagh Mountain. The chief witness against him—it was that poor silly creature, Bridget Dolan."

A few weeks later a man named Garrett Nowlan was executed for the murder of John Mason—more than four miles from Ballynultagh. Again the witness was "Croppy Biddy."

Though Anne always assured her father that they were doing fine, the household of women and children was like an army without a general. The potato crop that year had been satisfactory, but they were unable to resist the pleas of neighbors even more unfortunate than themselves. When their supply ran low, they sometimes ate nettle soup, like the cottiers' families. Their clothes had grown shabby. Rent was overdue, and only because of the unusual patience of Mrs. Darby were they allowed to stay on.

In all this time, no formal charges had been made against Bryan Devlin. "He should present a petition, demanding either a trial or a discharge," Mrs. Darby advised them. The petition was duly submitted and finally, in January of 1801, two years and three months after his arrest, his trial was held at Rathdrum. The whole family—their mother, Julie, Mary, Anne, Little Arthur, John, even Nellie and Jimmy—attended, as did many of their neighbors.

Bryan Devlin was brought in, handcuffs on his wrists, and taken to the prisoner's dock. He was haggard, his black beard now streaked with gray, but there was about him a dignity that set him apart from other men. They could not afford a lawyer for him, nor had it occurred to them he would need one. There was no one in county Wicklow who could speak one word against him—or so they were convinced.

The prosecutor presented his case. He pointed out that the nephews of the prisoner were all outlaws. He mentioned that the prisoner's wife had shown "undue sympathy" to the "criminal Terence Byrne" on the date of his execution. Even in such a prejudiced court, neither accusation was sufficient to condemn a man. Then the prosecutor announced he had two witnesses.

The first, Tom Halpin, Mrs. Darby's gardener, stepped up and was sworn in. Seeing him, Anne remembered that not once since their father's arrest had Halpin stopped by to see if they needed anything. Now he testified that in May of 1798, Bryan Devlin had brought to his house the two armed rebels, John and Terence Byrne. He also swore positively that Anne's father supplied money and provisions to his outlaw nephews, which was, of course, false.

The second witness was an even greater shock. Anne heard her sister Mary gasp. She had recognized this slender, good-looking young man before Anne did—Terry's brother, John Byrne. It was the practice of the courts to condemn a prisoner to death, then grant him amnesty if he turned state's evidence. Anne did not doubt that John Byrne was testifying to save his life, but this knowledge did not lessen her contempt.

It was to his credit that he tried to be evasive, but as the prosecutor continued to bombard him with questions, he also swore that Bryan Devlin had supplied sustenance to his outlaw nephews.

Instinctively Anne reached out and pressed Mary's hand. Her sister returned the pressure.

"Don't worry, Anne," she said in a soft almost inaudible voice, "He was a winning youth who could make a woman feel a special, beloved creature. But even from the first I knew he lacked the solid substance of his brother."

Anne felt a great relief. She should have had more faith in Mary's good sense—the good sense of a Devlin.

But the trial was going poorly for her father. "He will likely be deported to Australia," whispered a neighbor.

"Bryan Devlin, do you have anything to say in your defense?" demanded the judge.

Bryan Devlin stood silent a moment, as though gathering his thoughts. "A man should not be asked to defend his own character," he said at last. "To do so would be a sign of pride, a sin that God himself condemns." However, if the judge felt need of learning more about him, he would refer him to Magistrate Thomas King, President of the Court. "I can appeal to no gentleman who knows me better or longer."

Had times been normal, Anne would have been confident that her father's old friend would rise to his defense. But since her father's arrest, Magistrate King had become Commander of the Rathdrum Corps of Yeoman Cavalry, and no one was more assiduous than he in trying to cure "liberty fever" by "bloodletting." She was certain he would not favor a known relative of the insurgents. But Magistrate King proved a truer friend than Tom Halpin.

"I have known the prisoner from our youth," he said. "I know him to be a very well-conducted person. Residing close to his residence, I have had every opportunity of knowing his habits, and I frequently saw him attending to his business, particularly in the time of the rebellion. I cannot admit the testimony of these witnesses. The prisoner had no opportunity to assist the rebels in the manner sworn to."

After this statement, the judge had no alternative. Bryan Devlin was acquitted, a man free to join his family.

They took him home with them, laughing, crying, chattering like blue jays all the way. Nearly all the food in the house went to a banquet of celebration. For Jimmy and Nellie, his reappearance was a revelation. They walked around and around him, their eyes never leaving his face. As for him, he was gay as Anne had never seen him, talking and singing until very late in the night.

The next day he was up at dawn and at work. His expression grew more and more grave as he saw the run-down state of the farm, and found out the extent of their debts. He made no reproaches, but one morning he left early and did not return until dusk. Then he gathered them around him.

"I have arranged to sell some of our stock and pay the arrears on the rent," he said. "I have also turned in my lease to Mrs. Darby. Today, at Rathfarnham, a few miles south of Dublin, I took a lease on a small dairy farm. There we will try to forget all that has passed."

The next day, Anne rode across the mountains to say good-by to Mary and Kathy Dwyer and, through them, to her outlaw cousins. A light snow had turned hills and vales into a white wonderland of almost unbearable beauty. The farewells were sad and her heart was heavy at the thought of leaving friends and relatives. Part of her would always remain in county Wicklow, with Terry Byrne and the other martyrs of '98. But already at the age of nineteen, she possessed an earthy realism that enabled her to accept what cannot be changed and to look forward with curiosity to the future.

7

The Coming of Robert Emmet

The word "rath" means fortress, and the many towns in Ireland whose names thus begin are said to be the site of ancient fortresses. No trace of them now remained, and in moving from the neighborhood of Rathdrum to that of Rathfarnham, the Devlins were simply making a change from a mountainous country to level land. From their doorway on clear days they could see the blue hills of northern Wicklow and the granite domes of the more distant mountains; to Anne it was at once tantalizing and frustrating to be forever within sight but out of reach of her homeland.

By 1803 they had lived two years on their dairy farm. They owned cows, chickens and several horses. The two-story stone farmhouse had an enormous kitchen, where they lived and ate, and where Mary, Anne and Julie took turns in making butter in the barrel-shaped wooden churn. They sold butter, as well as eggs and milk, and raised crops sufficient for their needs.

Bryan Devlin also worked as a carter, carrying supplies for neighboring gentry to and from Dublin. John and Little Arthur, husky young men of sixteen and eighteen, worked with him, and were now well trained in all the varied skills of a farmer. Nellie and Jimmy were old enough to gather eggs, feed the chickens and do other simple chores.

They had all worked hard and had prospered. Meat was on their table several times a week instead of only on festival days. With lengths of cloth which their father brought back from Dublin, the girls made their own clothes—capes and dresses, which were pretty and becoming if not as elegant as those of the rich. There were white linen sheets and warm blankets on their beds.

Arriving as strangers, they had won the esteem of their neighbors for their industry, their readiness to be of service, for the modesty of the daughters and the polite behavior of the sons. They were adults, but their father's word was still law. He forbade them to join in village sports or dances held at local fairs, saying that such activities were destructive to the morality of the young. They accepted his discipline as they always had done, but at home among themselves they were as boisterous and full of fun as young people anywhere. Theirs was an unusually close family, bound together even more firmly because of their father's long imprisonment.

Yet for all their normal, pleasant family life, they, like others who had gone through the '98 Rebellion, found bitterness an undercurrent with which they had to live. The wounds caused by injustice, personally experienced, are not easy to heal. By nature, Anne was, as Mrs. Heppenstall had once described her "cheerful and willing and quick to learn." The lessons she had learned during the Rebellion had gone deep. Had she not seen her virtuous father languish in gaol for no reason at all? Could she forget that John Byrne had gone free for betraying his benefactor or the sight of Terry Byrne, who had stood true, being led to his death? And could one accept, what now seemed undeniable, that all their sacrifices had been vain?

Since 1800, Ireland as a separate country had ceased to exist. That year, the British-controlled Irish Parliament had voted its own dissolution, its members yielding to the bribes of Lord Cornwallis. Irish industry was strangled by the grip of a thousand English-imposed rules and regulations. The Irish peasantry and working class, Protestant and Catholic alike, were still plunged in misery.

Her family's relatively comfortable state could not blind Anne to the sad fate of her country.

"What is wrong with us?" she burst out one evening in March, as the family were gathered around the hearthside.

"Wrong?" Her mother looked up from the pair of blue worsted stockings she was knitting for John. "What would you be meaning, Anne?"

"Must we always live as a conquered people?" she continued passionately. "Must we go on doing nothing? Ah, if I were a man, I would want to be like Michael Dwyer and never lay down my arms!"

"Anne, you frighten me when you talk like that," protested her sister Mary. "Women are not meant for fighting."

Her father drew on his clay pipe, emitting a cloud of smoke. "Some women are and some women are not," he said thoughfully. "When I was in the Wicklow gaol, I heard a story about a French lass who did a bit of fighting for her country. Her name was Joan. They called her Joan of Arc. I do not know just why."

Bryan Devlin had heard many stories during his incarceration, which he produced, one by one, like precious jewels won at great cost. They all settled down to listen.

"Joan was a farmer's daughter," he said, "a simple girl without education. She lived about two hundred or more years ago, when France, like Ireland today, was overrun with the English. A good and devout Catholic she was too, and once when she was in her garden, St. Margaret and St. Catherine came down to chat with her, saying she was to save France. Promptly she took off to the King and repeated what the saints had said. He never doubted it was true and gave her a suit of shining armor and the most beautiful white steed in the world. The English, when they saw a woman heading the French Army, turned and ran like frightened sheep." He paused.

"Did the King marry her and make her his Queen after the English were driven out?" asked little Nellie.

Her father shook his head. "Alas, no. 'Tis a true story and true stories are all too likely not to have a happy ending. Joan was taken prisoner by French soldiers—those who, like our yeoman and militia, had joined with the English against their own. They denounced her as a heretic and burned her at a stake. There are those who say that the heart of Joan of Arc would not burn even with the great heat of the flames. I could not say for sure, since I was not there."

He shook the ashes from his pipe, as a signal that the story was over.

"Let's go outside and play," Nellie proposed to Jimmy. "I'll be Joan of Arc and you can be the French soldiers who take me prisoner."

"Why must I be the French soldiers?" he complained, following her all the same.

Anne sat on by the fire dreaming. If only she could do for her country what Joan of Arc had done for hers! But then it was not granted to everyone to hear the voices of the saints. She herself had never been so favored.

The children rushed inside pell-mell.

"There's a sailor outside," announced Jimmy. "He asked if Bryan Devlin lived here."

"He did?" Their mother paused midway in her knitting. "What did you tell him?"

"We said we knew no such person," spoke up Nellie. "We thought maybe he was coming to arrest Father again. He looked so unhappy that I said I would come inside the house and see if there was anyone here who had ever heard of Bryan Devlin. He's sitting on the doorstep now. He said he had walked from Dublin and was too tired to go any farther."

" 'Tis a strange world," sighed their mother, "where babes in arms must be suspicious of strangers."

Bryan Devlin rose and went outside. He returned with his arm over the shoulder of the visitor. In the late dusk they did not recognize him at once.

"What's the matter with you?" their father bellowed at them. "Aren't you going to give my brother's son a proper welcome?"

"Big Art!" Anne cried out incredulously. Her mother jumped up to embrace the guest, saying, "Well now, I should have known you anywhere by that mop of red hair." Then the whole family was welcoming him, except for the little ones who could not remember him and only stared in awe. Mrs. Devlin made him sit down at the table and promptly brought out a basket of potatoes and cold meat left over from their supper. From the way he consumed them, it was clear he had been eating irregularly.

Ah, but it was good to be among one's family once more, he told them, to smell the sweet musky fragrance of a turf fire. But what changes there were since he had been with them last—nearly five years before. Little Arthur now—he grinned affectionately at his namesake and godson—a man full grown. John as tall as himself. The little ones he had left as babies—pushing up like young trees. And Mary, Julie and Anne—he looked them over like a connoisseur—sweet and luscious and pretty enough to have every lad in the countryside on his knees before them. But then the Devlins always had been a handsome lot. If 'twas himself who said it.

"You always were the cocky one of the lot," said Mrs. Devlin, laughing. She was the only one present who had no Devlin blood.

"Are ye in trouble, lad?" Bryan Devlin asked abruptly.

What trouble could a man have, he asked with a shrug, other than knowing that if the yeomen caught up with him he would be tortured and that if the English did so, he would be hanged? But then that sort of trouble was nothing new.

It was evident he had much to tell them but did not know how to begin.

"On with it, lad," said their father, relighting his pipe. "Say what you have come to say."

Big Art got up and stood by the fireplace, facing them. Did they know that under an assumed name he and his brother Pat had enlisted in the British Army? No, they wouldn't, since it happened after they had left Wicklow. Some forty or fifty other Wicklow rebels had joined up too.

It had seemed a good idea at the time to let the British pay for their keep and give them proper military training too. They had been sent to the south of England, where Pat had joined the Fleet, hoping to get to America. There was no telling when, or if, he would ever return.

"And yourself, Big Art?" Anne demanded. "What are you doing in sailor dress?"

A disguise, he said, lest he be recognized and picked up. He had deserted the Army, and had persuaded his Wicklow companions to desert with him. They had made their way to Liverpool and thence to Dublin.

"And for what reason?" asked Bryan Devlin.

He was coming to that, he said. While in England, he had met some Irish patriots, returning from exile in France. They told him of plans for a new Irish uprising. The leader was one Robert Emmet, younger brother of the celebrated United Irishman, Thomas Addis Emmet. Thomas Addis, exiled after his imprisonment, could never return. His young brother was taking over now. In France, he had even gained an audience with Napoleon, regarding French support. Now he was in Dublin, getting matters organized.

"Be you telling us, nephew, that you risked so much to serve a man on whom you'd never set eyes?" demanded Anne's father.

"Aye, I did."

"Was that not rash?"

"It was a feeling I had. It was the way the men looked who had known him, all glowing with hope and confidence. When I came to know him myself, I knew he was a man I would follow until death."

"What is he like, this Robert Emmet?" Anne asked.

"He is young, he is educated, he is a Protestant. His heart

is aflame with love of Ireland and his spirit afire to set her
free. He was brought up in luxury, and though his inheritance is small, he has given it all for our cause. More than
that, you must wait to meet him. He is now seeking a place
outside of Dublin to make his headquarters. . . ." He dragged
this last sentence out into a question mark.

Anne waited breathlessly to see what her father would
say. His belief that if he remained a peaceful man and
minded his own business there would be nothing to fear
had been rudely shattered in '98. What would he do now?

He deliberated only a moment. "Tell Robert Emmet that
we will gladly have him stay here with us, should he so
desire."

Anne gasped with pride. She should have known that her
father was no less a hero than her rebel cousins.

Two evenings later Big Art returned. "I have brought
Mr. Emmet."

The stranger he presented to them looked younger than
his twenty-five years. He was slender, pale, with regular
features, slightly aquiline nose, dark hair and large dark
melancholy eyes. His attire was plain—brown whipcord
breeches, brown jacket, white waistcoat and neckpiece, high
Hessian boots. Anne had expected that the man whom her
cousin had voted to "follow until death" would be more
impressive, and she felt disappointed.

He shook hands with them all, patted Jimmy on the head
and ruffled Nellie's red curls in the manner of an adult with
a special tenderness for children, told them that he knew
through Big Art of their ordeal in county Wicklow and that
he counted it an honor to meet such a courageous family.
He spoke hesitantly and it struck Anne that he was shy,
perhaps almost as much so as her sister Mary.

He was grateful for their offer of hospitality, he went on, but could not take advantage of it. Wherever he was, there would be men coming and going, day and night. Such activity would make them too conspicuous, leading certainly to trouble for them. What he needed was a large house in a secluded spot, out of sight of the main road to Dublin.

"But there is just such a house not half a mile from here and it is vacant!" exclaimed Anne. "It is on Butterfield Lane, which winds through bushes, sycamores and beeches. There are several other houses on the lane but they are well set apart from each other."

"There is? That sounds splendid, Anne." He smiled at her, and as he did so, his whole face became radiant. "Big Art and I will look into it tomorrow."

He stayed to take a cup of tea with them. With Bryan Devlin, he spoke of the scores of taxes that weighed on every farmer, peasant and worker in Ireland. With Little Arthur and John, he discussed military strategy—about the need for a plan in any battle attack and how, with a good plan, a small detachment could outwit a more numerous enemy.

He launched into stories of Irish history, speaking of Brian Boru, the ninth century king who drove the Danish invaders from southwestern Ireland; of Feagh MacHugh O'Byrne, the great Irish chieftain whose castle was in county Wicklow's Glenmalure Valley, and whose clansmen had passed down the name "Byrne" to so many Wicklow citizens.

As Robert Emmet talked on, his whole personality changed. From a retiring and formally polite young man, he became transformed to a dynamic human being, whose words, vibrant and eloquent, rang out with a life of their own. Anne wondered how it was she had not noticed what a beautiful voice he had when first he spoke.

He was talking now of modern heroes, of their cousin, Michael Dwyer, of Sam McAllister who had given his life for Dwyer, and of Billy Byrne of Ballymanus. Did they know of the ballads being chanted about these men, in secret, in every corner of Ireland? "Their deeds will be taught to Irish schoolchildren everywhere—once Ireland is free again."

Could there be anything more thrilling than to hear one's neighbors and relatives assigned an important place in Irish history? The Devlin family listened in raptured silence. Mary was weeping openly.

"I know how Big Art feels," Little Arthur said solemnly after their guest's departure. "I too would follow him until death."

Mrs. Devlin folded up her knitting. "I do believe," she remarked quietly, "that if Robert Emmet were talking to a field of stones in Connemara, those stones would all get up and join him in his revolution."

Big Art came to see them again the next day. He and Mr. Emmet had inspected the house on Butterfield Lane and found it satisfactory. Robert Emmet had leased it under the name of "Mr. Ellis" and would move in within a few days. He would need a housekeeper for the cooking and cleaning. Big Art had suggested that Bryan Devlin might permit one of his daughters to work there.

"Mary is not suited by character to stay with strangers," their father said thoughtfully. "Julie is too young and frivolous. Anne, would you care to help out Mr. Emmet?"

"I would and gladly." She spoke quickly before her father could change his mind.

If she could not, like Joan of Arc, lead her country to freedom riding a white steed, she was not going to refuse the chance to serve in a more humble capacity.

F

8

Butterfield Lane

For the next three days, Anne spent most of her time at the Butterfield Lane house, scrubbing the floors, washing windows, polishing woodwork. Julie and Mary came over to help her, taking turns bringing in water from the well. Little Arthur showed up with a spade and some bags of seed.

"What is that for?" Anne demanded.

"I thought I would pose as Mr. Emmet's gardener," he said. "Every gentleman should have a gardener. I talked with Big Art and he agreed it was a good idea."

Before Anne could comment, he went through the house and out into the rear to start digging the ground. His efforts inspired Mary and Julie to plant hollycocks and roses and other flowers in the front yard. "It makes the place more cheery."

John walked in with some eggs and butter. "Mother sent these, to give you a start in filling up the larder, Anne. Father is bringing over some potatoes and meal later in the day."

Bryan Devlin brought the provisions in a cart, freshly painted blue, drawn by one of their best work horses. John returned with him, leading a cow.

"I'm leaving cow, horse and cart here," Mr. Devlin said gruffly. "Mr. Emmet may have need of them. Besides, they will show the neighbors that he has a business."

Robert Emmet came to see how preparations were going.

"There's not a speck of dust anywhere, Anne," he commented admiringly. "We will move in tomorrow."

"I suppose your furniture will be arriving?" she asked.

"Furniture?" He looked blank. "Oh, yes! Big Art is bringing some straw mattresses."

"And chairs and tables and beds?" Anne pressed him.

He shook his head. "We will have to find some boxes or crates for the time being. Anne, we shall need every shilling for blunderbusses and pikes."

She asked him what he liked to eat.

"What do you propose?"

Her notions of the proper food for such as he stemmed from her period in service at the Heppenstall mansion on Inchicore Road.

"Quail, lobsters, roast turkeys?" she suggested.

His eyes widened in astonishment. "Tell me, Anne, is that what you eat at home?"

She admitted they ate plainly—potatoes, garden vegetables, pork or boiled beef, occasionally fish. "But Mr. Emmet, the gentry live differently. You cannot be expected . . ."

"And why not?" he interrupted her. "Do you really think, Anne, that the gentry, as you call them, are constructed of finer materials than peasants or farmer or workman? I assure you they are not. Prepare what you would eat at home, and we will be more than satisfied. The important thing is that costs be kept low."

When he came back the next day, he brought with him a big, handsome gentleman with dark curly hair.

"This is Thomas Russell, Anne. He is going to share our quarters."

The newcomer bowed in a courtly manner. "I am charmed to make your acquaintance, Anne."

She was overwhelmed. This was the man who, with Wolfe Tone, had founded the United Irish. Worldly and sophisticated, he had deserted all his gay companions of pleasure, sold his commission as an army officer, and toured Ulster and other places in Ireland, preaching the cause of Irish unity. He had spent several years in prison and then, like Mr. Emmet's older brother, had been exiled to France. Yet he had elected to return and serve under a man at least ten years younger than he.

Mr. Russell and Mr. Emmet slept in the two upstairs bedrooms. Anne took for herself a small room off the front hallway, its only furnishing consisting of a straw mattress and a few shelves which Big Art put up for her personal belongings. Often Big Art stayed with them too. He was working part time for Mr. Grierson, the King's printer, who lived nearby, but his real job was manager of Butterfield Lane. He pretended to be Little Arthur's boss, and was often out in the garden telling him how to raise vegetables—as though Little Arthur did not know as much as he about farming.

Two other young gentlemen moved in with them—William Dowdall, a former newspaper publisher, and William Hamilton, Thomas Russell's nephew. For the most part, their visitors were workingmen: Jemmy Hope, a kindly little weaver; Henry Howley, a big, hot-tempered carpenter; Nicholas Stafford, a baker; Henry Hevey, a brewer; bold and charming Miles Byrne, a Wexford rebel who had been working incognito as a bookkeeper; Michael Quigley, a bricklayer from Kildare; two other Kildare men, Thomas Wilde and

John Mahon. Nearly all this "inner circle" of Mr. Emmet's were veterans of '98, and some had served prison terms.

In spite of Little Arthur's garden and the presence of the cow, horse and cart, the neighbors grew more than curious about "Mr. Ellis," about his strange assortment of friends, his house furnished only with straw mattresses and crates.

"They are debating whether he is a counterfeiter or in hiding to escape debtors' prison," Big Arthur said, chuckling. Neither he nor anyone else in the Devlin family gave these neighbors any satisfaction. Once at the Rathfarnham market, a woman cornered Anne. "What profession does Mr. Ellis follow?" she demanded bluntly. "Is he an attorney?" "Aye, is he?" said Anne, and walked off.

She learned that William Hamilton, who was young and flirtatious, was calling on the daughters of a Mr. Frayne, who lived next door. In the evenings he walked with them in their garden, joking and laughing. She scolded him roundly. "You should be ashamed, spending your time so foolishly when serious matters are at stake."

"But Anne, I did not tell them anything they should not know," he protested.

"Maybe you did not. But when one talks at all, there is always a chance that one talks too much."

Abashed, he agreed to be more careful.

The virtue of caution was deeply impressed on all who had been through '98. Sometimes when Anne passed through the room where the men were talking, those who did not know her lowered their voices or fell silent.

"Fear not. She is one of us," Mr. Emmet reassured them. "We can trust her as we would ourselves."

Never had she so cherished a compliment.

Living and working at Butterfield Lane, she could not help

knowing what was going on. Mr. Emmet had leased an
empty building on Patrick Street, across from St. Patrick's
Cathedral in Dublin, and another on Thomas Street, both as
depots to store pistols and blunderbusses and ammunition,
purchased mostly from his own inheritance. Men were working in these depots too, constructing pikes, preparing explosives, and a special rocket which Robert Emmet had
invented. They were an army. They had to have arms.

They had to have men too. Jemmy Hope, the weaver, was
organizing his own trade and other working-class Dubliners,
among whom he was well known, loved and respected. The
exuberant Thomas Russell went up to county Ulster, his
home territory, to round up those whom he had signed up
years before in the United Irish Society. Miles Byrne brought
rebel leaders from counties Wexford and Carlow to meet
Robert Emmet, confident they would go back and rouse
their old companions of '98 to readiness for a new struggle.
This was Mr. Emmet's scheme, to confide in only a few, but
to prepare the men all over Ireland to rise when the time
came.

"Tell me about your cousin, Michael Dwyer," he asked
Anne one evening.

"What can I tell you that you do not know?" she demanded. "For five years now the English have failed to track
him down. How he lives, what he does, I have no idea.
Probably the country people give him food and shelter, and
I am sure if he said the word they would follow him."

A few days later Big Art and Jemmy Hope set off on horseback to see Dwyer. Take me with you, Anne wanted to
plead, remembering the gorse and bracken and heather in
the wild wilderness of Imaal. Instead, she told them with her

usual tartness to be careful and do nothing to arouse suspicion.

They came back a few days later, stomping into the kitchen, tired, hungry and depressed. They made their report to their chief, while Anne served them dinner.

"Did you see him?" Mr. Emmet asked.

"Aye, we saw him," said Big Art.

"What did he say?"

"He said it was unlikely that the men of Wicklow would take up arms again, that it would be more than difficult to convince them to risk another failure."

"Did you ask Dwyer to meet with me here?" Mr. Emmet demanded.

"Aye, we did. He said he might. He would not set a date. He said it would be within two or three months."

Just three days later, Anne was wakened late at night by a rattling at the door. Sleepily she rose, pulled on her petticoat and bodice, and lit a candle.

"Who is it?"

A deep voice gave the password they all used.

She opened the door and saw a huge and burly figure standing there.

"Hello, Anne." It was Michael Dwyer.

Excitedly, she bade him come in, led him to the drawing room, made him sit down on one of the crates they used as chairs. "'Tis a pleasure to see you all in one piece."

"Not quite." Grinning, he help up his left hand, which had only a scar where his thumb had been. "You remember Tom Halpin, the gardener who turned informer."

"He did that to you?"

"That scum! He would be afraid to shoot a rat. He brought

a troop of soldiers to seek me out. I fired at him—but my
most ancient firing piece went off in my hand."

Robert Emmet, a light sleeper, appeared at the head of
the stairway.

"Who is there, Anne?"

When she told him, he was down the stairs with a bound.
Then the two men were shaking hands, the one big and wild
looking in frieze coat, corduroy breeches and heavy boots;
the other slim and aristocratic as a young prince.

"I'm glad you were able to come, Dwyer. We have need of
you."

"I'm making no promises," Michael said grimly.

"I know. You came alone?"

"My men are with our horses waiting outside of Rathfarnham. They'll join me if I don't signal them otherwise.
Who is in this house besides yourself and Anne?"

Mr. Emmet named Thomas Russell.

"I've heard him well spoken of. Who else?"

He mentioned Dowdall and Hamilton, with a few words
about each.

Michael Dwyer grimaced. "I'll take your word for them.
But mind, no one is to leave as long as we stay, unless it's
Anne or yourself."

"As you wish, Michael Dwyer," Mr. Emmet promised with
his slow smile.

Anne, thinking her cousin might be hungry, brought in
some bread and cheese. He shook his head. All he would
accept was a tankard of porter. When the call of a whip-
poorwill sounded almost beneath their window, he nodded
to Anne. "There they are. You let them in, Anne."

She opened the door to welcome her other cousin, Hugh
Vesty Byrne, no longer a youth but a man, rugged and

weather-beaten. He walked with a limp, the result of a thigh wound which had never been properly tended nor completely healed. With him were Martin Burke, the man whose escape from prison was being celebrated the night she visited Imaal, and John Mernagh, another six-footer, a dark man, older than the others, with heavy eyebrows and a complexion pitted with smallpox.

"I have brought with me the three most trustworthy men in Wicklow," Michael Dwyer said.

"Are you hungry?" Anne asked them.

When they admitted they were "near famished," she prepared a midnight supper, which they devoured to the last morsel. Again, Michael touched nothing. Anne retired to her room presently. The men were still talking when she arose. She persuaded Hugh Vesty, Burke and Mernagh to stretch out on some mattresses in an inner room for a nap, but Michael Dwyer would have none of it.

"I never sleep in a strange place. That is perhaps the only reason why I still have my head on my shoulders."

Periodically all day long he strode over to the shuttered windows and peered outside. During his entire stay, he ate almost nothing, drank a moderate amount of porter, slept not at all. His conduct gave Anne a hint of what he had gone through, living five years like a hunted animal.

On the third day he and Mr. Emmet came into the kitchen for a private conference.

"Shall I go?" asked Anne, who was making supper.

"You shall stay," said Michael firmly. He turned to Mr. Emmet. "My little cousin has nerves of iron and the blood of a patriot in her veins. Would she have told you about the stormy night when she and my sisters under the noses of the yeomen carried the body of poor Sam McAllister to the churchyard, so he could have a proper burial with his comrades?"

"She would not," Mr. Emmet shook his head, smiling gravely. "Anne is one who talks little except to rebuke us when we are late for meals or go out with buttons missing or our boots unpolished."

"Get along with your business," Anne said. She bent over to stir the fire so they would not see that she was blushing, more pleased than she would admit to have Mr. Emmet know that her cousin held her in high esteem.

Soon they were deep in conversation.

"I've been playing hide and seek with death for a long time," she heard Michael tell Mr. Emmet. "The seal of doom is on me and all I can do is to stall the black lady as long as she is willing. But I'm not going to lead my men into a trap. It's not enough for someone to say, 'Arise and we will be free.' That's been tried before, and in vain. Can you understand, Emmet?"

"I understand all too well." Mr. Emmet's voice was low and earnest. "I will outline what we have in mind. For several months the gates of Dublin Castle have been left open until far into the night." (Dublin Castle was the seat of the British-controlled government and had become a symbol of oppression to the Irish.) "There is only a small guard on duty and the Viceroy and his secretaries walk about unprotected. Our first detachment will ride inside in a line of hackney coaches. Under their greatcoats they will carry blunder-busses and pistols and a special pike we have contrived which can be folded up to less than three feet. It should be a simple matter to take over the guard and make the Viceroy a prisoner, after which we will fire off rockets to call in other detachments. If only five thousand respond—and there are sure to be many times that number—Dublin Castle will be in Irish hands."

"And when the British send their forces to recapture the Castle?" Michael demanded.

"They most certainly will do so," Mr. Emmet said, "but by the time they arrive, the Castle gates will be closed and we will have them at a disadvantage. In the meantime, the news that the green flag is flying above the Castle will have inspired the whole country to join us."

This was the first time Anne had heard in so many words Robert Emmet's basic plan for the uprising, and she was impressed with it. What would her cousin think? He was pacing the floor, his hands behind him, his forehead lined with thought. It was apparent that in spite of his mighty will power, he was fighting a losing battle with sleep. Shaking his head to cast out the cobwebs, he said slowly, "It might well work. One should not be overlooking that much might go wrong. . . ."

"I am aware of that." Mr. Emmet rose. "Our efforts are to see that there is enough redundancy in any one part of the plan to make up for deficiency in any other. I leave it to you to decide whether you will join us, Captain."

"I have decided," Michael said abruptly. "This much I will tell you. When you have been in possession of Dublin for forty-eight hours, we will bring five thousand men. You can count on that."

They joined the others in a glass of claret to clinch the agreement. Before he raised his glass, Michael walked once more to the window and peered out through the shutters. A woman was standing before their house.

"Who is that?" he demanded.

"Only a neighbor," Anne explained. "The women around

here are great gossips. They think Mr. Emmet is a counter-feiter, and sometimes they put their ears to the ground to try to hear his presses."

Her cousin was not amused. "We stay in no house that is being watched," he said and ordered his companions to pack their equipment and be ready to leave as soon as dusk fell.

Anne and Mr. Emmet walked out in the fields with them to the clump of trees where they had tethered their horses.

"As soon as we have the Castle we will signal you by mountain flares," Mr. Emmet said as he shook hands in farewell.

"There's only one signal that will have meaning for us, Robert Emmet," Michael told him. "That is the sound of a cannon."

"The sound of a cannon it shall be—if it is in our power," he agreed.

"You can be proud of your cousins and country friends," he told Anne as they walked back through the early twilight. "They are certainly as excellent as they are clever."

"They are at least large enough to be good," Anne said, choking.

9

Sarah Curran

That a man such as Robert Emmet, reared in a fine house with many servants, should give his heart and soul and all his worldly goods to the cause of Irish freedom, aroused in Anne a constant wonderment. On her visits home, she could not keep herself from quoting him, talking about him, singing his praises.

Never had she met a man of such learning. He spoke French and Latin and also Gaelic, the language of the Irish people in many parts of the country. He knew about chemistry and mathematics and was an artist—it was he who had designed the seal for the United Irish—and wrote poetry. . . .

As a young boy he had attended meetings of the United Irish with his brother, Thomas Addis. He had organized a branch of the society at Trinity College when he was only fifteen—but had sent in his resignation to the college rather than swear allegiance to the British Crown. . . .

It was a beautiful way he had of speaking of Ireland, as though their country were a lovely woman, whom every man could be proud to protect. It was thrilling to hear him talk of the right of all men, and women, too, to their share in the earth's goodness, to liberty and freedom from persecution.

In all the time she had worked for him, not once had he addressed her as a servant. He was kind, generous, wise. Not once had she seen him lose his temper, which was more than could be said of herself. . . .

"I do believe, Anne," said Julie, listening to one of her hymns of praise, "that Robert Emmet has taken your heart."

"Have you gone daft?" Anne cried.

She was furious with her sister for suggesting there was anything personal in her devotion. Nor had it struck her as odd that with all the men coming to Butterfield Lane, most of them young, many of them handsome, all of them brave enough to risk their lives, not one other had taken her fancy.

"Mr. Emmet belongs in a different world from us."

"Why?" persisted her sister. "Because he is gentry and we are not."

"No. Because he is the noblest creature that ever walked the green earth," Anne stated flatly.

"Anne, darling, for your own sake, admit he's but human," Julie pleaded. "All men have their weaknesses."

"Not he," Anne insisted loyally. "His heart belongs to Ireland. He has no room in it for common mortal passions."

She found out, not long afterward, how wrong she was in that latter statement.

He came into the courtyard a few mornings later, as she was hanging out clothes to dry.

"Anne, I have a great favor to ask you. I wonder if you would deliver a letter for me. Not far—only about a half a mile from here on the road to Dublin—at the big yellow stone house called the Priory, which belongs to Barrister John Philpot Curran."

"Aye, I know the place." She was puzzled by the hesitancy with which he made this ordinary request. Barrister Curran was one of Ireland's outstanding lawyers, one of the few who had thus far been willing to defend Irish patriots. He was also an old friend of the Emmet family. There was nothing surprising in Robert Emmet sending him a letter.

"The letter is to the barrister's daughter, Miss Sarah Curran," he continued, his eyes not meeting hers. He handed her the envelope. "I would like you to deliver this personally into her hands. Would you do that for me?"

"I will." Her first thought was that Miss Curran must be working for his conspiracy, though that seemed odd since he had not mentioned her before.

She picked up her laundry basket and headed back into the kitchen. He followed her in.

"Anne, I want to explain."

"You've no need to explain anything to me."

"I must, Anne. You should know that I love Sarah Curran —so much that sometimes I feel I cannot bear it. Her father found out how I feel and has made it clear I am no longer welcome at his house. He is quite right. No man ever had less to offer a wife. I should stop seeing her but I cannot. I know I am not being fair to her. . . ."

And are you being fair to the men who believe that your every thought and act is for the success of the uprising? She could not voice this reproach, with his dark eyes on her, begging her to understand.

"I want you to meet her, Anne. She is kind, she is lovely— and heaven only knows how good. I know you will like each other. I want you to be friends."

And since when does a highly placed young lady seek out

the daughter of a farmer for a friend? She did not express
this doubt either.

Later that afternoon, with mixed emotions, she raised the
brass knocker of the big house known as the Priory, a charming place set back from the road, surrounded by a spacious
lawn and flower gardens. Dressed in her best, a black cotton
gown trimmed with a frilled triangular white collar, a white
lace-trimmed bonnet and black leather shoes, Anne wondered why the maid who answered the door eyed her with
distrust. Perhaps because she had not arrived in a carriage,
she told herself.

"I would like to see Miss Sarah Curran. Tell her that Anne
Devlin is calling."

"I'll see if she is busy." The servant closed the door in
her face, leaving her standing outside like a mendicant.

Almost immediately a young woman flung it open again.

"Anne, how glad I am you came!" Her voice had the sweet
high tone of twittering birds. "I have been so hoping you
would be here today."

Sarah Curran was about her own age and height. Her
auburn curls reached below her shoulders and her skin was
fair with a few freckles across her nose. She was not beautiful, but even at first glance Anne was aware of the charm
that had enchanted Robert Emmet. She wore a filmy white
high-waisted dress which clung to and molded her graceful
figure.

"Do come in." She led Anne into the hallway. To the servant, standing by disapprovingly, she frowned and stamped
a tiny silken slipper. "Maggie, next time my friends come
calling, do not leave them standing outside. You were fearfully rude. Now bring us tea up to my room. And cakes and
marmalade and biscuits—stacks of them."

"Truly you need not bother with the tea," Anne said as they walked up the wide spiral stairway.

"But you must stay, Anne. I am so bored, here alone all day. I want to talk with you. Robert won't mind, I'm sure he won't."

The room into which she took Anne was as feminine as she, with fragile gilded chairs upholstered in flowered tapestries, a carpet as soft and thick as mountain moss, lace curtains at the windows, cushions everywhere.

"Sit down here." She indicated a silken divan and took her place at Anne's side. "Robert has told me everything about you except *comme vous êtes jolie*—how pretty you are! But then he would not notice anything like that, his mind being so filled with his revolutions and uprisings."

"He sent you a letter, Miss Curran." Anne took it from her bodice and gave it to her. She had a peasant's distrust of flattery and had not made up her mind about Mr. Emmet's sweetheart.

"Dear Robert!" Sarah caressed the letter with white slender hands that had never washed clothes or dug weeds or performed any other menial chores. "I will tell you something odd, Anne. When I first met him, at a ball about a year ago, I did not care for him at all. He was so serious and shy and stiff. I think it took all his courage to ask me to dance. I simply did not know what to say to him. Every young man knows how to dance, but not Robert. It must have been the first time he had even tried." She burst into laughter at the memory of it.

The maid came in with the tea tray.

"Set it down, Maggie," Sarah ordered her imperiously. "I will serve. You need not wait."

G

"Yes, Miss Sarah." The servant placed the tray on the low table before them. "Will you be needing anything else?"

"If I do, I will ring." Anne would have been repelled by Sarah's manner, reminding her of the treatment servants received at the Heppenstall mansion, had not she added repentantly, "I did not mean to sound curt, Maggie darling, but Anne is a very dear friend of mine and I simply must talk with her alone."

"I understand, Miss Sarah." The maid's tone held unmistakable tenderness, and she went out happy.

"Maggie has been like a mother to me since my own mother—left us," Sarah said. "Sometimes she becomes over-zealous and then I am unsupportable. Not that I blame her, my mother, I mean, for walking out. Our house had been dreadfully gloomy ever since Gertrude died. Gertrude was my younger sister and my father's favorite. In fact I don't think he really loved any of us but Gertrude. He shut himself up in his room and ignored us, as if we were to blame that she fell out the window. *Elle en avait assez.* That means Mother could not stand it. Do you know French, Anne? I think it is a blissful language. Naturally I don't speak it as well as Robert. *Pas possible.*

"Do tell me, Anne, how dear Robert is. He works so dreadfully hard. I started to tell you how I happened to fall in love with him, did I not? It happened when Papa made Amelia tell him not to come here any more. Amelia is my older sister. I thought it was fearfully ill-mannered of Papa, and I had to see Robert to tell him so. We met down by the river but no one knew about it except Amelia. I had never seen him alone before. Always there was Papa doing all the talking. When he started to tell me how deeply he felt about me, I thought I would swoon. He does have a beautiful voice, does he not, Anne?"

"Aye, he does." To keep up with Sarah's rapid shift of subject matter was as exhausting as trailing after a race horse.

"Let me serve you some more tea. And take some more cakes. I wish you would eat all of them. Maggie sulks when anything is left. She frets constantly because I have no appetite. I suppose you can tell that my health is delicate." She pouted. "That's what the physician tells you when he means you will die young of consumption."

"I did not know," Anne cried out in undisguised distress. "Surely you are mistaken."

"I'm quite sure. Don't fear. I have said nothing to Robert. He suffers too much because of me as it is." She unclasped the slim golden chain she wore around her neck, slipped a locket from it, which she opened. "Let me show you something, Anne. A lock of his hair and a lock of mine—woven together. Until death do us part." Suddenly her eyes filled with tears. "It's too horrible to think of death, is it not? Tell me, Anne, you do think his revolution will be a success, don't you?"

"I hope so."

"You say that as though there were a chance it would not be." Sarah grasped Anne's hand and looked at her searchingly. "I could not stand it if anything went wrong. Robert is so *sure*. He's not in any danger, is he?"

Anne was nonplused. Was it possible that this daughter of a liberal lawyer believed that anyone, even Robert Emmet, could plot to overthrow English control of Ireland and not be in very grave danger? Then it occurred to her that Mr. Emmet must have assured her at some length that what he

was doing was no more hazardous than a game of cricket.
If so, it was not up to her to say otherwise.

"I am sure Mr. Emmet is capable of taking care of himself."

"I am glad to hear you say that, Anne. He has planned
everything so carefully. Those depots on Patrick Street and
Thomas Street. All those blunderbusses and pikes and
pistols. It makes me laugh to think of the expression on the
Viceroy's face when the hackney coach passengers jump out
and take him prisoner!"

"He told you about that?" Anne gasped.

"But of course, Anne, dear. Robert and I have no secrets
from each other. When we cannot see each other, Robert
writes to let me know how everything is progressing."

"He writes you . . ." Anne stopped lamely in the middle
of her sentence.

Sarah smiled, like a mischievous child. "How shocked you
look! I know what you think but you are mistaken. We are
tremendously careful. We've made up our own secret code.
Nobody—not even the cleverest person—could figure out
what we are talking about."

"All the same," Anne counseled her, "I think you should
find a safe place for his letters—or better still, destroy them."

"Your guest is right, little sister. You do take far too many
chances."

Anne turned to see another young woman standing in the
doorway. She was as strait-laced in appearance as Sarah
was full of coquetry, dressed in shirtwaist and skirt, her
hair combed in a severe knot.

"Amelia, how long have you been here?" Sarah demanded.

"Just long enough to hear your last words," her sister said.
"I came to tell you that Papa is home and waiting for you

in the parlor, extremely indignant that you are not downstairs to greet him."

"I'll go right away. Amelia, I've been crying a little. Will Papa ask questions?"

"He will not. He is much too upset at present about what his defense of Irish rebels has done to his precious career to notice anything we do."

"How cynical you are!" Sarah exclaimed reproachfully. "You know Papa will always be an Irish patriot."

"'Always' is a word not to be used rashly," Amelia said. She turned to Anne. "Don't you agree, Miss . . ."

"Anne Devlin," interposed Sarah. "She is Robert's closest confidante. Has she not the most beautiful soft, dark hair and blue eyes? Don't you think I should be jealous? Imagine, Amelia! She sees him every day."

"Sarah!" roared a deep voice.

"You had better descend at once or he will be up here," Amelia commented. "I will show Miss Devlin out."

"Oh, I hate to see you leave. Please forgive me, Anne. I had hoped we would talk for hours. And would you give Robert my letter?" She whirled around and took an envelope addressed in a dainty handwriting from a red sewing basket. "Tell him it is sealed with my kisses. Do come back soon." Impulsively she threw her arms around Anne, then ran from the room, calling, "I'm coming, Papa."

"My sister is a child," Amelia said somberly, as she escorted Anne down a hallway to a side entrance. "I worry about her. But then I suppose I should not. Don't you believe, Miss Devlin, that it is better to know love, however briefly and however tragically, than never to know it at all? I speak as a spinster who has never had a suitor cast a glance in her direction."

She apparently did not expect an answer to this question, nor could Anne think of one to give her.

Mr. Emmet was standing at their doorway when Anne turned into Butterfield Lane. He was down the steps in one stride to join her.

"You saw her, Anne?"

"I did. I had tea with her. I gave her your letter and she has sent one to you."

He took the letter but his eyes were on her face. "What did you think of her?"

"I think," Anne said slowly, "I think she has the mildest and the softest and the sweetest look I ever saw."

Seeing his expression of gratitude, she knew that she had done right to hold in abeyance her reservations. Within herself, she harbored an odd sort of jealousy, ill-defined and never expressed, as though she, Anne, was the woman Ireland, and Sarah, a beguiling temptress who would lead her savior astray.

10

Shadow of Catastrophe

As plans for the uprising came to a climax, Butterfield Lane was invaded by an increasing stream of visitors. They usually arrived after dark, talked all night, sometimes leaving before dawn, sometimes not until the next night. It was not exceptional to have thirty or more for dinner, meaning far more work than Anne could handle alone. Though the guests and boarders offered their services, they were all thumbs, like most men when they attempt women's work.

In the emergency, Jemmy Hope's wife Rose came down from Dublin to help out. With her, she brought her four-months-old baby; she had three other children whom she had left with neighbors. Jemmy had been immersed in revolutionary activities since the beginning of their married life, she confided to Anne. In all those years they had never been able to hear a knock at their door without misgivings, and they had narrowly missed arrest more times than Rose could count. She had remained cheerful as a cup of hot tea, saying that having a husband like Jemmy was worth all the trouble he caused her. Her presence was a tonic for Anne, who was delighted to have another woman to talk to in this household of men.

There was a feeling of exultation at Butterfield Lane those first days of July, which summer rains and thunderstorms could not dampen. Even their chief often hummed to himself, usually off key, and frequently there was an odd half-smile on his lips. Their plans, he told Anne, were going splendidly. Favorable reports were coming in from all over Ireland. The people were ready and waiting to rally to the call of liberty.

Anne's family were now in the conspiracy up to the hilt. Big Art was on the go every waking moment. The ardent youth who had set off for Newtonmountkennedy, his musket over his shoulder, five years before had become a man of formidable energy, his tall frame lean and hard as a rock.

Little Arthur, who had just passed his nineteenth birthday, was their most trusted messenger. That he looked younger than his years lessened the risk of detection, and his strict upbringing nullified the hazard of his being waylaid in local taverns. Impressed with his clear handwriting, Mr. Emmet had also made him his secretary. In the beginning he dictated letters and messages to him; later he merely told Little Arthur what he wished to say and let him compose them. For the first time since the departure of his schoolmaster, he had a chance to satisfy his thirst for knowledge. Mr. Emmet kept him well supplied with books from his own library, and whenever he had a few moments to spare he gave him personal instruction.

"Who knows? Maybe, when Ireland is free, I can continue my studies after all and qualify myself to teach," Little Arthur bragged to Anne, half embarrassed to admit the revival of his childhood dream.

"When Ireland is free . . ." The phrase was one they were all using those days, without ever a qualifying "if."

Bryan Devlin had sometime since decided, with what inner struggles Anne could only guess, that young Robert Emmet was worthy of his full support. The cart which this gray-bearded patriarch drove through the streets of Dublin was often loaded, not with farm produce, but with weapons, ammunition, and timber for making pikes. Several times he and Big Art had been to county Wicklow, bringing ball cartridges and gunpowder and new guns to Michael Dwyer and his men, to replace their antique weapons such as the blunderbuss with which Michael had shot off his own thumb.

On their last visit they had carried along four uniforms, with white pantaloons and green jackets, made in the Thomas Street depot by a tailor named Colgan. They were gifts from Robert Emmet to Michael Dwyer, Hugh Vesty Byrne, Martin Burke and John Mernagh, the four who had visited them. For Michael Dwyer had now agreed not to wait forty-eight hours after the green flag was floating over Dublin Castle. He wanted to be notified the very day the uprising was to be schedued.

Only Anne and a few others knew that the date—July 23 —had already been set.

Anne had taken more letters to Sarah Curran, and little by little that blithe friendly soul had succeeded in winning her heart. Her first doubts about this romance had been quieted. She assured herself that if Mr. Emmet had confided his plans to his beloved, he must know what he was doing, and it was not her place to judge him. Without Sarah, she realized now, the terrible responsibility which the young brother of Thomas Addis Emmet had taken on his slender shoulders might have been more than he could bear.

They were no longer counting on French aid. Though England and France had technically been at war again since May, Thomas Addis had sent word from Paris that Napoleon had lost interest in Ireland's fate.

"We will manage without him," Anne heard Robert Emmet tell Thomas Russell. "I still do not trust Napoleon and would prefer to call on him only as a last resort." His tone implied that he thought it unlikely there would be need of a "last resort."

On July 16, Anne and Rose were alone most of the day, and took the opportunity to do a thorough housecleaning. In the afternoon they went out and did some gardening, leaving the baby on a blanket nearby to catch a little sunlight. It was a peaceful, pleasant, promising day. Afterward they prepared dinner, but no one, not even Mr. Emmet, showed up. Well after dusk, Little Arthur came rushing in.

"There be bad news," he gasped. "An explosion at the Patrick Street depot. One of our men was killed and two were wounded and carried off by the police. The building is badly damaged."

"Dear God in heaven!" murmured Anne, sinking down on a stool. "Who were the unfortunate men?"

It turned out that she did not know them, but that did not lessen her horror. At least half their ammunition was stored in Patrick Street. The police, and the men at the Castle, must certainly be making an investigation. All their careful preparations seemed doomed.

Little Arthur stayed with them that night, sitting up late to read by candlelight Thomas Paine's *Rights of Man*—the essay that had given so much inspiration to Irish patriots.

Reading was his way of forcing worry from his mind. In their separate rooms, Anne and Rose tried to sleep but it was no use. About two o'clock Anne rose and made tea for the three of them. They were in the kitchen sipping it gloomily, when they heard a cart drive up. It was Big Arthur, who looked almost cheerful.

"We have a job to do," he announced. "Little Arthur, get your spade." He poured himself a cup of tea and drank it like a man dying of thirst. "My cart is filled with all the makings of a revolution. We must hide them before it gets light."

He and Miles Byrne had gone to Patrick Street as soon as it was dark to assess the damage, he told them. To their astonishment, no one was on guard. The place was deserted. Inside, they found that the police had taken all their tools, some explosives and a stack of pikes, but the secret cupboards, built by Michael Quigley under Mr. Emmet's direction, where most of their arms and ammunition were stored, had escaped their attention.

He and Miles had taken as much as they could carry on their persons to the Thomas Street depot. A hostler, John Fleming, who worked for the adjoining White Bull Tavern, provided them with heavy sacks. Those sacks, filled with pistols and cartridges, they had carried across Dublin in half a dozen trips, emptying them with comrades who could be trusted.

Only once had they been stopped—and then by a couple of night police who demanded what they were doing. They had managed to outwit them and escape but had decided to take no more chances. All that was left they had packed into the cart which Big Art had brought to Butterfield Lane.

By dawn he and Little Arthur had buried most of it in the garden, while Anne and Rose replanted the uprooted vegetables that now sprung directly from weapons of war. The rest they hid in the barn and the attic.

"But why would the police leave the depot unguarded?" Anne demanded incredulously.

"Stupidity," said Big Art. "That's the only reason I know of."

The *Dublin Evening Post* carried only a small paragraph about the explosion, saying that, though alarmists had not been idle, inquiries had revealed nothing of a political nature connected with the event.

"It doesn't make sense," Rose Hope puzzled. "In my long experience, police inquiries always bring forth something of a political nature—even when there is none."

From Little Arthur they learned that Mr. Emmet and the other leaders were reassured and had voted to go ahead as scheduled. Anne did not see her employer all that week. He was staying in Dublin those last frantic days. He had innumerable details to attend to—more than could be done had he a staff of a thousand, Little Arthur told them. The loss of the Patrick Street depot, even though so much material had been salvaged, was a serious blow.

Anne missed seeing him more than she would admit. It seemed to her that if she could hear him speak, just once, in his eloquent and modulated tones, the fears which the explosion had engendered would vanish. When Rose was called back to Dublin because of the sickness of one of her children, she felt more alone than ever.

Saturday, July 23, dawned cloudless and clear. Anne was up at dawn doing the washing. The sun was warm on her back as she hung her clothes out to dry. About seven, Robert Emmet arrived on horseback. He looked as though he had not slept or eaten for the week of his absence, but his expression was serene.

"Good morning, Annie. I came to see if I had any messages."

"Aye, you do." The mere sight of him had set her heart soaring.

There was a batch of letters, including one from Sarah Curran. He came into the kitchen with her, read most of his mail rapidly, burning it thereafter, but thrust the note from Sarah into his waistcoat pocket.

"I don't have much time, Anne."

"I know." She poured out a basin of warm water for him. "You'd best clean up."

"How right you are." He slipped off his coat, rolled up his sleeves and scrubbed his face and arms. "I'll do you full credit later in the day. Colgan has finally finished our uniforms."

"You need a clean shirt, Mr. Emmet. There's one on the line but it's not yet dry."

"There is? That's fine." He rubbed himself with a towel. "Would you do something for me, Anne? Would you bring it into Dublin? Meet me at the Thomas Street depot about noon. Sometime this morning I'll write Sarah a letter. I'd like you to take it to her."

Anne promised she would do so, thinking that in all the world there was no woman more fortunate than Sarah Curran.

Big Art walked in. "I've come for my orders, General."

Mr. Emmet laughed. "Your general would like you to pick up William Kennedy at the Yellow House and go with him to Rathcoole, Athgoe and Hazelhatch. Tell our men there that we expect them in Dublin this afternoon. Then join me as soon as you can. The attack will begin at dusk."

"Will that be all?"

"No. Stop by at Red Michael's place and have him set out at once for Wicklow to notify Michael Dwyer to come in haste."

"I am off, General," said Big Art. He turned to Anne. "There's a fine sound to that word 'general,' is there not?"

Excitement and fear were seething within her like an ill-assorted brew, but she forced herself to think of household matters.

"We're running low on meal, Mr. Emmet. I wondered how much I should order."

"Yes, yes," he said absent-mindedly. "Go ahead . . ." Leaving the sentence unfinished, he went into the next room to collect some papers.

"I'm going now, Anne," he called.

She went outside with him. As he mounted his horse, he smiled down on her fondly. "Good-by, Anne."

She watched him until he was out of sight, as she had done a hundred times before. Strange how little different it seemed from any other day.

11

July 23, 1803

Bryan Devlin drove Anne as far as the New Market in South Dublin where he was delivering their butter. From there, it was only a short walk to the Thomas Street depot.

As always on a Saturday, Dublin was crowded with rattling market carts and herds of bleating sheep and bawling cattle, urged forward by the shouts of their drivers. She was in the slum area, streets narrow and foul smelling, lined with rickety gabled houses with gaping paneless windows. Grimy urchins played heedlessly beneath the hoofs of passing horses. Ragged women clutched whimpering, hollow-eyed infants in their bony arms. Taverns—of which Dublin had more than two thousand—spewed out their staggering, bleary, quarrelsome clients.

"The misery of Dublin is equaled nowhere in the world," Anne had heard Mr. Emmet say. It was his conviction that hunger, drunkenness, brutality, ignorance would all vanish once the Irish were running their own country for the good, not of the few, but for everyone. She stepped gingerly over the slime and filth, her heart filled to bursting at the thought of their "general" who would that day be leading his people to a better life.

She approached the depot by Marshalea Lane, which led to the back entrance. To reach the door she had to edge her way through a stream of wagons. From inside the depot came a fearful din, banging and hammering and shouting. Men, many in country clothes, were gathered in groups, talking loudly. She stepped aside for two men who were carrying a load of wooden beams—beams which she knew were hollowed out to hold pikes. With a spasm of dread, she realized that any outsider could not help being suspicious at such unusual activity.

"Where the devil did you put the fuses?" she heard someone cry out. Then she saw Michael Quigley, the tall, lanky bricklayer, come out of the depot, deep in a dispute with a companion about some missing fuses. She ran up to him.

"Is he inside?" she aswed. "I have brought him a shirt."

He looked at her in bewilderment as if he had no idea what she was talking about. Finally he grasped who she was. "Why, no, Anne, he isn't here. You might try in the White Bull."

She started to ask him to deliver the shirt to Mr. Emmet, but just then some man ran up with a question about scaling ladders.

"Thank you kindly, Mr. Quigley," she told him, but he was already moving away.

To get to the White Bull Tavern, she retraced her steps and went around the corner. The tavern adjoined the depot and provided another entrance to it. Since the police never ask men their reason for entering a tavern, the proximity was a definite advantage. Moreover, the proprietor, Mrs. Dillon, was a loyal patriot and they could count on her cooperation.

Still Anne entered reluctantly. A tavern was not a place to be visited by any respectable woman.

It was hot and crowded and the air was filled with the smoke of pipes and the heavy odor of porter. Anne cast a quick glance around but saw neither Mrs. Dillon nor Mr. Emmet. The clients, gathered at the bar or tables, did not even notice her presence as she moved along the wall to a hallway where she could stand unobserved. Several roughly dressed men were seated only a few feet away, and she could not help hearing their talk.

"What brings you to Dublin, Pat?" one said to his neighbor.

"I be here to find me an apprentice," the other responded gravely.

"As for myself, I came to buy hops," said the first.

"And I to see a man about a gamecock," a third explained his presence.

"And I to consult a doctor about my aged grandmother who has been having chills and fever this last fortnight," broke in a fourth. "Fancy the strangeness that we should all be arriving the same day!"

These then were the men who had come to Dublin from some country village, using one excuse or another, but really to join Mr. Emmet's army. Rough they might be, but their hearts too were beating for freedom!

As she watched, another man came over to them.

"Would ye mind if I join you?"

"The space is free."

"I see ye be in Dublin for the same reason that brought me here," said the stranger, sitting down with them. "It must be a disappointment to you as to myself that the whole thing is postponed a week."

H

"Be ye speaking the truth?" "Are ye sure of what you say?" The men piled questions on him.

"As sure as I am that my mother's lying in her grave. The one they call the general—it was a shock to discover he was no more than a babe—he's postponed the whole affair."

Anne could not have kept still if St. Peter himself had ordered her to do so.

" 'Tis not so! You are a liar," she said, stepping forward.

"And who might you be?" The man she had accused turned toward her, but without giving her time to speak further, shouted, "Begorra, there's a lass to take a man's eye away from his proper wife. Come here, my pretty." Then he had his arms around her.

"Leave me be, you ruffian," she burst out in fury, struggling to free herself. All too well, she saw that he was trying to distract attention from her accusation. The big fellows nearby understood too and rose.

"An informer, is he? We'll take care of him."

They closed in on him as she fled down the hallway. She landed in the stables, where John Fleming, the hostler, was giving feed to the horses.

Fleming was the one who had provided sacks for Big Art and Miles Byrne on the night of the explosion. He was a simple round-faced youth with the air of one not in complete possession of his five senses, but Mr. Emmet had sent him to Butterfield Lane several times with messages for her and she was sure he could be trusted. She explained what had happened and asked if he had seen "Mr. Ellis," as most of the men knew him.

"He was here not so long ago," he said, scratching his head. "I think he was off to buy up more blunderbusses for the Kildare men who said they would not fight with pikes.

If you'll go inside and wait for him, he'll likely be coming in soon."

"I'll not go back for any price." She handed him her basket with Mr. Emmet's shirt and some other things for him. "John, give this to him when he comes. But more important, pass along word that there are troublemakers around. I don't think the one in there will do more harm, but there might be others."

"Aye, Anne," he promised obligingly.

She left, only half satisfied, but knowing she had done all she could. Halfway to the New Market to meet her father, she remembered the letter Mr. Emmet wanted her to take to Sarah Curran. Ah well, it was too late for that now.

Back at Butterfield Lane, John, whom she had left in charge, told her there had been no visitors. The place was quiet as a graveyard.

"Is everything going well, Anne?"

"Everything is going well." She spoke mostly to reassure herself, to blot out her anxiety about the undue commotion around the depot, the undue drinking in the tavern, the informer, and the blunderbusses the Kildare men were demanding at this late hour. "Father wants you home to do the chores, John. You had best be going."

Reluctantly, he departed. He would have loved to be in the thick of things, like Little Arthur, but their father had insisted he needed one son for the heavy work around the farm. Anne sympathized with his disappointment but was glad there was one adult male in her family she did not need worry about that day.

She had no idea where Little Arthur was. Big Art must be in Dublin at his post by now. Her father had gone off on some mission. They were all, as she well knew, in imminent danger. All afternoon she wandered restlessly around the big and empty house. Just when it seemed to her she could bear the suspense no longer, in walked little Nellie, fresh and sweet in a new white dress.

"Mother said I could stay all night. Will you tell me a story?"

Until the child's bedtime, she told her tales of leprechauns and banshees and other wee folk whom some country people believed to be as real as the pig in the sty or the chickens in the coop. After Nellie fell asleep, she went down into the kitchen and baked some cakes—more to keep herself occupied than because she expected anyone home to eat them.

Around ten o'clock, a Wexford man came to collect the remaining cases of gunpowder stored in the barn. He volunteered no information and she knew better than to ask for any. As they were packing up the powder in the kitchen, she heard voices outside.

"You had better get out the back way. Make haste."

He hesitated at the door. "And you?"

"I will be all right. Go now." She practically shoved him out the door.

Straightway the front door opened. It was not the militia but Robert Emmet himself, with five of his men—Michael Quigley, Henry Hevey, the brewer, Nicholas Stafford, the baker, the two Kildare men, Thomas Wilde and John Mahon. All wore their uniforms—white pantaloons, green jackets trimmed with gold lace, cocked hats—but there was no grandeur about them. Their faces were lined with fatigue and downcast with defeat.

Her relief at their safety was fast followed by blind anger that they should be there at all.

"What have you done?" she cried out. "My bad welcome

to you. Have you destroyed the whole kingdom and all belonging to me? What has become of your preparations? Are they all gone and lost?"

"Don't blame me, Anne," Mr. Emmet said wearily when she paused for breath. "The fault is not mine. Everything went wrong."

"And where are my brother and cousin?" she continued mercilessly. "I suppose you have left them among the dead. I don't know what Little Arthur would do, but I know my cousin would not run away."

Thomas Wilde, a big gentle man, drew her aside. "Don't be making things worse for him than they are, Anne," he pleaded.

Briefly, he recited the day's long list of disasters, some evidently the result of sabotage, others of plain misfortune. The crowning blow came when Quigley, who was on guard, had mistaken some strange men for soldiers and had rushed into the depot crying that the army was coming. Although they were not ready, Robert Emmet had decided it was better to fight than die in a trap. They had slipped into their uniforms, thrown stores of arms out the window to their men and then started out.

Worse, they had gone on foot, the hackney coachmen having been frightened off by an accidental inquiry from a British officer. By the time they reached Thomas Street, their number had shrunk from three hundred to fifty. At Patrick Street, only a handful were left. It was then that Emmet had decided he was leading them only to their death, and called a halt.

"It is all over then?" asked Anne sadly.

"Yes," he said.

The men talked in low voices. Scraps of their conversation

reached Anne as she went back and forth, trying to get them to eat something or drink some tea to bring back their courage.

"It should have succeeded," Mahon kept saying over and over. "It should have succeeded."

Mr. Emmet sighed. "Had we another week, another thousand pounds, a thousand more men—we would have had nothing to fear. Unless . . ." His voice had a bitterness in it Anne had never heard before. "Unless the Castle knew about us all along."

"Impossible!" said Wilde. "If that were so, why were we not stopped?"

"For the same reason they provoked the Rebellion of '98." His look was anguished. "To smoke out the Irish patriots. Probably none of us will ever know the truth of it."

Anne's anger against them had passed. Her heart bled for them all, especially for Mr. Emmet, but she could not stand by and see them act sorry for themselves.

"What is past cannot be changed," she burst out impetuously. "There's no use dwelling on it. You have to think what comes next."

"Anne's right," said Mr. Emmet looking at her in amazement. "We must not believe that all is lost. They will certainly get our ammunition and pikes at Thomas Street but we still have firearms. We know that the spirit of the people is high. If the French could now be persuaded to send an expedition, we would have a good chance."

As he spoke on, his men stopped slumping and their dejection vanished. Even at this moment, when morale was lowest, Robert Emmet had not lost the power to instill confidence in those around him. Yet Anne knew, as well as anyone, how very slim was the chance of French aid at this point.

They could not stay at Butterfield Lane. It was practically certain the place would be searched.

"Do you have a place to go?" she asked them.

"Yes, we have friends in the country," Mr. Emmet assured her.

"With daylight coming on bright and strong," she exploded, "you would be riding down the roads wearing your uniforms that can be seen a mile? Have you all lost your senses? You had best cross the fields and go to my father."

"It is not fair to him, Anne," Mr. Emmet protested.

" 'Tis too late to be thinking of that now. Have you gone through your papers and destroyed those that might endanger you?"

They hadn't. A long shred of rose was on the eastern horizon by the time they had finished this task.

"Get going now and hurry," she urged them.

"You must come with us, Anne!"

"I will not. Someone must remain to warn our country friends, should they show up." Michael Dwyer was still expected. There might be others.

"You'll be in danger if you stay."

"They won't hurt a woman." She would not be argued from her decision.

Soon after their departure, Big Arthur showed up, white-faced beneath a coat of grime.

"I have seen death and destruction, Anne. The men whom I persuaded to desert with me—there are those among them who are lying lifeless on Francis Street."

"Little Arthur?" she asked.

"I sent him on home."

She burst out sobbing.

She sent Big Art over to her father, as well as several others who straggled in that morning. That day and the next she kept Nellie with her. "If anyone comes asking questions," she warned the child, "tell them nothing." But there was no more visitors until the next evening when Julie came over to see how they were.

"Our walls are fairly bursting with rebels," her pretty young sister told Anne excitedly. "I know that 'tis a tragic thing, but what a sight to see Mr. Hevey with my apron around his waist, churning butter! Only something dreadful happened."

"What was it?" Annie demanded anxiously.

"Our neighbor, Mrs. Donlevy—you know what a busybody that one is—walked in without knocking, took one look and left. She'd been gone but a few minutes when Mr. Grierson's butler rushed over. Mrs. Donlevy had arrived during dinner to announce that Bryan Devlin was harboring fifty French officers! Had not Mr. Grierson liked to eat so well, he would have left at once for the Castle. Father had time to get some horses for the men. They have just gone . . . Anne, what will happen to us?"

"I don't know," Anne said. "All I can say is that we must be prepared for the worst."

12

The Half-hanging

From the upstairs bedroom where she and Nellie were sleeping, she heard the rumpus below, the shouting, stamping of boots, doors slamming, the sound of heavy objects being overturned. It was Tuesday morning, three days after the beginning and the ending of the uprising. In an instant Anne had pulled on her blue cotton skirt and white blouse.

"What's happening? Who is making all that noise?" asked Nellie, sitting bolt upright in fright.

"Lie down and be still. There's nothing to fear," Anne said soothingly. "I'll be right back."

Halfway down the stairs, she saw the intruders, a score or more armed yeomen and a man in civilian dress who she learned later was a magistrate. They were tearing around like the Seven Furies, searching corners, upsetting everything.

"What are you doing here?" she blazed at them. "This is a gentleman's house."

"Seize the girl," an officer shouted.

His men grabbed her roughly and pinioned her against

the wall, pointing their bayonets at her. Early as it was, they were obviously half drunk.

"Where is Mr. Ellis?" the officer demanded.

"I don't know." She made her expression stupid. "I'm only the servant maid here."

"You lie. Was he here last night? Where did he go?"

"Where he comes from, where he goes to, it's nothing to me as long as my wages are paid," she said saucily.

The magistrate strode up to her. He was an elderly man in tall hat and long frock coat. "Mr. Ellis," he announced, "is a conspirator against His Majesty's government. A letter addressed to him was found in a desk in a warehouse on Thomas Street. The warehouse was filled with ammunition intended for a bloody attack on the authorities."

"I know nothing of that."

"Maybe this will refresh your memory?"

She winced with pain as a soldier jabbed his bayonet in her side. "Leave me be!"

Several of them came down the stairs, dragging Nellie, still in her chemise.

"Anne, they wouldn't let me put on my frock," she wailed, as though this was the greatest catastrophe in the world.

The officer grabbed her by the shoulders. "Tell us the names of the men you've seen in this house."

Nellie stared at him sullenly. "I know no one here except my sister."

"You lying spawn." A soldier jabbed the child in the chest and a bright red spot appeared on her chemise.

"You scoundrels! Leave my sister alone!" Anne tried to push her way through her captors, but they held her firmly.

"Come, come," said the magistrate in an oily voice. "You

have no need to be afraid. Just tell the truth. Where is Mr.
Ellis?"

"I know nothing about him."

"Give us the names of his visitors."

"I never asked them."

The magistrate wagged a long bony finger in her face.
"You are as deeply involved as they. If you won't tell everything you know, you will be publicly hanged, and that before evening."

All of them were yelling at once now, demanding the
names of the "conspirators."

"No, no," she cried out, goaded beyond endurance. "I will
tell you nothing as long as I have breath in my body."

"That's enough," the magistrate said, his face bloated with
rage. "We will hang her—here and now."

They pushed and prodded her out into the courtyard,
along with Nellie, who was bleeding profusely from her
wound and still begging to be allowed to put on her frock.
While several men guarded the child, the others took Anne
over to the bright blue cart which her father had loaned to
Mr. Emmet. Two soldiers tilted it up and threw a rope over
the shaft, tying one end of it around Anne's neck.

"This is your last chance," the magistrate told her. "Say
where Mr. Ellis is and we will set you free."

"You may murder me, but not one word about him will
you ever get from me."

She tried to pray but had only time to murmur, "Lord,
have mercy . . ." when with a wild shout they pulled her up
and unconsciousness blotted out everything.

"Half-hanging" was a popular sport with the yeomanry.
They knew just how to tie a rope so that the victim's neck
would not be broken, and when to release the rope before

it was too late. When Anne returned to her senses, Nellie was leaning over her.

"Anne, wake up. The bad men are gone."

She pulled herself shakily to her feet and went into the kitchen. The sight made her shudder—crockery broken, cupboards upset, flour and sugar poured out on the floor. Even the water barrel had been emptied. Too weak to go for more water, she was trying to wipe the blood from herself and Nellie with a rag, when Mary burst in.

"We heard the shouts. I came as soon as I dared. Oh, what have they done to you?"

" 'Tis not serious," Annie tried to reassure her.

"The wretches should be drawn and quartered," sobbed her gentle, peace-loving sister.

Nellie pressed herself against her. "See, Mary, 'tis but a small hole." She showed the puncture in her shoulder.

Both older sisters wept then.

There was no use staying longer at Butterfield Lane. Michael Dwyer was apparently not coming. Anne closed and locked the door behind them, leaving forever the house that had for more than three months sheltered the dreams of the men who had wanted to make Ireland free.

It was not safe for her to stay at home either. When and if the Castle decided to investigate the "fifty French officers," Anne's presence would only further compromise her family. The day after her "half-hanging," stiff and sore as she was, she went to Dublin to stay with Michael Dwyer's sister Kathy, who was now living in the Coombe and married to a dairyman, a former Wicklow patriot named John O'Neil.

The O'Neils gave her a warm welcome, though it was risky for them to have her. Since the uprising, martial law had been declared in Dublin. Every house was required to post the name of its occupants. Unlisted persons were liable to arrest.

She had only a day to get reacquainted with Kathy when Little Arthur came to tell her that Robert Emmet wanted to see her. He had some messages for her to take to him and he had arranged for her to go with Thomas Wilde's sister, who owned a jingle, a funny little one-horse carriage. Miss Wilde was a prim and proper spinster, dressed in gray broadcloth, the last person one would suspect of having a rebel brother. In fact when they reached the guards, stationed now on all the roads leading out of Dublin, they were waved by without even a question.

"All Dublin is in a turmoil," Miss Wilde told her as they drove along. "Everyone is talking about the handsome young general who marched down Thomas Street in his green uniform trimmed with gold lace, his plumed hat, and his sword at his side. What a brave thing to do! What a foolhardy thing to do! They tell how he marched until his army melted away from him like butter under a summer sun, and he was quite alone. The story is an exaggeration, but that's what people are saying. Everyone is asking who that general is, the Castle being the most curious of all. Whatever happens, the name of Robert Emmet will live in history to inspire future generations. I am as sure of that as that today is Thursday, Miss Devlin."

Mr. Emmet and some thirty of his men were waiting for them on a wooded slope not far from Ballincascorney, several miles beyond Rathfarnham, looking far more like a band of masqueraders on a picnic than like men who would live in history. Big Art was with them, as well as Miles Byrne, and a number of others whom Anne knew well. With gusto they recited their adventures since she had seen them last.

They had spent Monday night with a farmer, John Doyle, nicknamed "Silky" Doyle. They had slept in the fields one night. They had gone into a tavern for something to eat, but some five hundred soldiers had come on a search party. The tavern keeper's wife, a remarkable woman, had shooed them into an attic room, then told the searchers that the attic flooring was rotting and they would risk their lives if they mounted there. Which was true in a sense, since Big Art with his blunderbuss was stationed at the door, ready to shoot it out with anyone who opened it!

These and other stories were related gaily, with many interpolations, as though being on the run was quite the most thrilling thing that had ever happened to them. Anne was not deceived. When they gathered around her, pressing on her word-of-mouth and written messages for their families and loved ones, she detected tears in the eyes of more than one of these bold warriors.

They had now decided to separate, each to go his own way. Big Art wanted to take Mr. Emmet to Michael Dwyer in Imaal, but he flatly refused, saying he was much too embarrassed to go near Dwyer after their failure. He was equally opposed to Miles Byrne's plea that he try to escape to France. "One thing shall never be said of me is that I abandoned the brave people implicated through my actions," he said.

He had a little money which he divided among them. Then he draped a dark cloak over his uniform, and after telling Anne and Miss Wilde he would ride part way with them, said a few words in final farewell to the men who had served him so loyally.

For Anne, their ride back was a mixture of bleak sadness

and exquisite joy—joy that she had been granted this brief moment at the side of the one who had come to mean so much to her, and sadness because of the separation she knew was inevitable. Ah, if their little jingle could be traveling through the years instead of over the miles—bringing them to an Ireland where there were no soldiers scouting the country for men whose sin was love of freedom!

Shortly beyond Rathfarnham, Mr. Emmet asked Miss Wilde to stop and let him out.

"Oh, Mr. Emmet, is that wise?" protested Anne. "This neighborhood is as full of informers as a kitchen with flies."

"Be reassured, Anne," he told her. "I have friends nearby who will shelter me."

And Sarah Curran within a stone's throw, Anne reflected.

The police came to the O'Neil house the next day, making a routine check. Anne was a superfluous person, they announced, since her name was not posted as a tenant. Kathy vainly insisted that Anne was there only to apply for a job as dairymaid with her husband. They arrested Anne and Kathy as well. John O'Neil, who had played a small part in Mr. Emmet's uprising and a substantial role in the Rebellion of '98, was left to guard the apartment.

The two women were kept four days in the Coombe guardhouse with some four hundred other "superfluous persons." Once they were visited by a stout man in full uniform with a large nose and a red face. Kathy told Anne that this was the notorious Major Henry Charles Sirr, the Dublin chief of police, a ringleader in the brutal floggings that had preceded the Rebellion of '98. Anne shrank into a corner and tried to make herself inconspicuous during his stay—not through fear of Major Sirr but because she recognized one of his escort as Tom Halpin. How the informer had gone up in the world! Happily, he did not seem to connect this Dublin "dairymaid" with the daughter of Bryan Devlin.

Eventually they were brought to an examining officer, who confiscated Anne's sewing kit—a thimble, a spool of thread and a needle—then told them they were free. All the way home Kathy and Anne laughed about this officer who considered a needle to be a dangerous weapon.

Letters were waiting for her, mostly from Mr. Emmet's followers in different parts of the country, who wanted to know what the situation was. Somehow she had become the key person of their shattered organization, the one in whom all could have confidence. She answered the letters as best she could and then burned them. One message was from Mr. Emmet, asking her to meet him at Mrs. Palmer's in Harold Cross, on the road to Rathfarnham. This was where he had stayed before coming to Butterfield Lane.

She was there the next morning. It was a big slate-colored house surrounded by a wall. The buxom Mrs. Palmer took her into the parlor which served as both bedroom and study for her fugitive tenant. He was seated at a table, a book before him, still in his fine uniform, his dark cloak thrown over a nearby chair.

"Thank you for coming, Anne. I know I have no further claim on your time."

She curbed her instinct to cry out that she would do anything in her power for him as long as she lived, and instead demanded sharply why he had not yet managed to find himself less gaudy attire.

He led her to the window. "I could not be more safe than there. If anyone comes, I will slip out the window, climb the garden wall, hide in the grain field on the other side until the coast is clear."

She was unimpressed and said so.

"Ah, if there were only more women like you in the world, Anne," he sighed. The next moment he was asking her to take a letter to Sarah.

As she walked toward the main road, she noticed a public house displaying a streamer labeled "Doyle's Tavern." Uneasily, she wondered if this Doyle was any relation to "Silky Doyle," with whom Mr. Emmet and his men had spent a night.

She found Sarah disconsolate and tearful.

"They won't catch him, will they, Anne? Oh, it is all too frightful."

Anne tried to comfort her as best she could.

"How I envy you for having seen him—even for a moment. How I wish I could go to him! Of course, it is out of the question. They won't think I had anything to do with the uprising, will they?"

"I am certain they will not unless you tell them," Anne said, more coolly than she had intended. It shocked her that Sarah would be thinking of her own welfare at such a time.

She stayed with the O'Neils about two weeks, continuing to do errands for Mr. Emmet and to act as go-between for his widely scattered "army." Then Little Arthur came to take her home.

"Jimmy has smallpox, Anne. He keeps crying for you. Father believes it safe for you to come. We have had no trouble from the Castle."

For the trip, he had hired a small closed carriage of the type known as a "noddy," so she could ride through Dublin

I

without being observed. It seemed droll to be so protected, after all the chances she had been taking.

She spent that evening at the bedside of her small brother. His head was clear but he was in pain and covered with sores, even on the soles of his feet. Smallpox was then a common malady and the danger of contagion was not fully realized. Many who should by all logic have caught it, did not. The rest of the Devlin family miraculously escaped.

It seemed wonderful to sleep at home again. In the last months she had had enough excitement to last the rest of her life. From now on, she told herself, she wanted nothing more than to stay with her family, do her chores, and live a peaceful tranquil life. However, it was not to be. Shortly past midnight, she was awakened by sounds that had become all too familiar, the stamping of horses' hoofs, officers shouting orders to their men, and then, inevitably, a banging on their front door.

Part III

A PRISONER

13

The Castle

It was raining that night, a chill, penetrating drizzle. With only the clothes on their backs, the prisoners were being marched single file across the fields, away from the farm which they had built up with arduous labor. The British soldiers and Irish yeomen were triumphant at their quarry —an elderly couple, three young women, two teen-age youths, and a small boy so ill with smallpox he could hardly stagger along.

Only Nellie had been left behind. She had buried herself under the covers, and had somehow been overlooked. John and Little Arthur had their hands bound behind their backs with the reins of their horses. Bryan Devlin had been similarly tied, but Anne had cut his bonds when the soldiers were not looking. He still held his hands behind his back. With their captors was a neighbor named Mr. Walker, who would brag that he had directed and escorted them to the Devlin farm.

At the Yellow House Tavern in Rathfarnham, the officer in charge called a halt. His men were demanding liquid refreshments as a reward for their night's work. Unceremoniously they shoved the prisoners inside. While the sleep-dazed tavern keeper brought out mugs of ale and porter, the Devlins, their clothes wet through, stood clustered together in a corner. Mr. Walker came over to them.

"I am truly sorry about this, Devlin," he said. "It is a very unpleasant affair. To prove to you that I am sincerely concerned about your welfare, I have resolved to hire a woman to look after your place and your cows until we see how matters go."

Hypocrite, muttered Anne under her breath. Her father made no sign of having heard at all.

The captain summoned a messenger to take a dispatch to the Castle. "Tell them we have taken the whole Dwyer family."

"To the devil with the Papists!" toasted a soldier, raising his drink.

"There's another across the way!" exulted his companion. "His sign reads, 'Patrick Murphy—Lodgings'! With a name like that, is there need for further proof?"

"Arrest Patrick Murphy!"

Several soldiers dashed out, returning with the lodge keeper, his son, a youth of Little Arthur's age, and two ragged tinkers, who had taken rooms for the night and who were now protesting volubly their interrupted sleep.

The wife of the tavern keeper came in to give her husband a hand with the unexpected customers. When she saw the plight of her neighbors, her eyes filled with pity.

"Is there something I can get for you?" she asked Mrs. Devlin.

"Nothing," Mrs. Devlin answered. "But there is one thing you can do. My child Nellie is at the house alone. . . ."

The woman nodded sympathetically. "Do not fear. I will see that she has a place to stay."

A yeoman came up to Bryan Devlin. "Have a drink!" He pushed a foaming mug toward him.

Bryan Devlin turned his head away proudly. Other yeomen and soldiers clammered around, insisting noisily that the male prisoners must drink with them.

"Very well. My sons and I will accept one drink." Bryan Devlin's tone showed that he agreed only to have some peace.

A soldier put his brew to her father's lips, but he scowled and reached up and took the mug. He had forgotten they believed him to be bound. He was promptly tied up, more tightly than before.

"I'll keep them from trying any more tricks," shouted the officer. "Cut their breeches, men. Then see if they try to run away." He guffawed unroariously.

The soldiers slit the breeches of the male prisoners down the back, so that they had to clutch them to keep them up, even though their hands were tied.

"Only a true gentleman could think up such a stunt," muttered Patrick Murphy's son.

They all bore this indignity stoically except the tinkers, whose violent blast of profanity was silenced only by the butt end of a musket.

"On the march!" ordered the captain.

With frequent stops at other taverns, the gruesome journey to Dublin took all day long. The rain never stopped. Late in the afternoon they were led through the gate to the Castle, a collection of imposing buildings built around a central enclosure. Anne and Julie were carrying little Jimmy between them. Mary was supporting their mother, who was near collapse. The taut faces of the men reflected the strain of their own ordeal of humiliation.

Watching for them as they entered was the bombastic Major Sirr, the Dublin chief of police whom Anne had seen for the first time in the Coombe guardhouse. At his side was Tom Halpin. "There's the greatest rebel in county Wicklow," she heard him say to his chief. He was pointing at her bearded father.

"Ah, Julie," she said softly to her sister, "and to think it was here that *he* dreamed of seeing the green flag flying."

Except for Jimmy who was taken away from them, the Devlin family was herded into a small bare room in the Tower, a place of detention where political prisoners were examined. Bedraggled, mud-spattered, shivering, coughing, wet to the skin, they sat on the floor, the women huddled together for warmth.

"If we could only speak of something not sad," sighed Anne.

"When I was a prisoner at Wicklow gaol, I heard a prophecy," her father began. He was sitting cross-legged and rubbing his hands to bring back the circulation.

"It is told among country folk in the South. They say that one day a giant will spring full-grown, a giant with red hair and two thumbs on each hand. When he stalks through Ireland, all the warriors buried in the ancient raths will rise from their graves and help him drive out the invaders.

"Have faith in this giant, my children. Know that whoever he may be, he will find his might and his power from those who have fought before him."

"Faith! 'Tis a beautiful word, Brian Devlin," Mrs. Devlin

murmured softly. "Whatever they do to us, let them not take our faith."

A guard opened the door. "Anne Devlin! Come along."

Anne rose reluctantly. She took one last look at her family —her parents, her two beloved sisters, Little Arthur and John. "I will be right back," she quieted their unspoken fears. Then she followed the guard.

He took her to another room. On the bare floor was her little brother Jimmy, with nothing but a woman's apron over him. He was breathing heavily.

She knelt down beside him. "Oh, my darling!"

Someone seized her and pulled her upright. She turned and saw a big brute of a man with little round eyes and a loose, lecherous mouth.

"What sort of a monster are you to leave a sick child like that?" she screamed at him.

In answer he struck her on the side of her face. To the guard he said, "You were a fool to bring her in here. Take her to Major Sirr."

The guard flushed but did not defend himself. When they were beyond earshot, he whispered, "That is Hanlon, the tower keeper. If you want to get along here, be pleasant to him."

"Never!" Anne said.

Major Sirr, resplendent in his uniform trimmed with gold epaulets, was waiting for her in his office.

"Well, Anne Devlin, so we meet again. You would have saved us trouble if you had identified yourself at the Coombe guardhouse."

So he remembered her! She made no comment.

He proceeded to ask a few trivial questions—how old she

was, where she was born, if she knew how to read and write. She answered correctly but briefly.

"We know that you know where the conspirators are," he said suddenly. "It will be better for you and your family—and your sick brother—if you tell us now."

She was silent.

"Well, Anne?"

"I know nothing about them. I was a servant."

"You are foolish to think you can deceive us." The major's voice was cajoling. "Your father was in comfortable circumstances. It is not usual for a person in his position to let his daughters go into service."

"My father has a large family. There were many mouths to feed."

He took out a monocle and stared at her through it. "If you care nothing for yourself, for your own self-respect, Anne, you should think of your family. What a fine thing it would be for them to be at liberty, provided for and protected."

"I don't know what you mean, sir."

"I will be frank with you, Anne. If you are a good girl and tell us where Mr. Ellis and his friends went after they left Butterfield Lane, I will see that you get five hundred pounds. That's quite a handsome fortune for someone like you."

She didn't hesitate. "If I never get a fortune save blood money, I will be without one all the days of my life."

"Blood money!" He assumed an air of bewilderment. "I don't know what you are talking about."

"You are asking me to be like Bridget Dolan."

"And who is Bridget Dolan? I don't know anyone of that name."

"That is strange," she said. "I thought everyone knew her. She is the one who gave information that led to the hanging of Billy Byrne of Ballymanus—and of many other innocent men."

"That's enough out of you," he bellowed at her. "You are a desperate young woman. I should keep you in gaol all the days of your life as an example for other women."

That night she slept on the floor of a tiny room without even straw to soften her slumbers. Early in the morning the guard let in a visitor—a tall, thin, dark gentleman with a handsome, dissipated face.

"Good morning, Anne," he said. "I am Dr. Edward Trevor, prison inspector and chief physician, agent of transports and deputy governor of Kilmainham gaol. I want you to think of me as your friend. Have you any complaints about how you have been treated?"

After the harshness of all those who had dealt with her since her arrest, she was overwhelmed at hearing a few kind words.

"Oh, your Honor, since you are a physician could I ask that you would look after my nine-year-old brother who is here and ill of smallpox?"

"There is a child of nine here? A sick child?" He looked profoundly shocked. "Certainly, I will do what is necessary."

"God bless you," she cried out in gratitude.

Her guard brought her a breakfast of bread and milk. "Make yourself presentable, Anne. You are to be interviewed by Chief Secretary Wickham, the most important official in Ireland next to the the Lord Lieutenant himself. A real gentleman, not like that bully, Sirr, or Trevor, the apothecary's apprentice who calls himself a physician. You should feel honored."

"It is an honor I could do without," she told him.

Her clothes were still damp. She cleansed the mud from her dark blue cotton gown as best she could, draped her red shawl around her shoulders, ran her fingers through her curls to arrange them in some sort of order—not to please her interviewers but for her own self-respect.

"You make a pretty picture all the same," commented her guard.

He took her into a magnificently furnished chamber, where from heavy gilded frames, former English prime ministers looked loftily down on her. Secretary Wickham, dressed in a velvet cutaway jacket and pleated waistcoat, and wearing a curled and powdered wig, was seated at a huge carved oaken table. Beside him was another gentleman with a large record book before him.

"Secretary Marsden and I want to ask you a few questions, Anne." In all of Ireland, there was no one more diligent in gathering data about Irishmen who were not pleased with English rule than Undersecretary Alexander Marsden. "We have already examined your family. You had better tell us the truth."

Their first questions were practically the same as those of Major Sirr the night before. A clerk wrote down her anwers.

"What is the real name of the man who called himself 'Mr. Ellis'?" Wickham asked then.

"I know nothing of that."

"Give us the names of the men who came to see 'Mr. Ellis.'"

"I do not know."

"One of them was Thomas Russell, was it not?"

"I cannot say."

They continued to try to batter down her resistance, now threatening her, now accusing her of risking the welfare of her family by her stubbornness. How could she, a simple farmer's daughter, hope to match her wits against these gentlemen, as skilled in extracting information from a rebel as a general in military strategy? "Dear God in heaven, please give me guidance . . ." she prayed inwardly.

Finally Marsden closed his book with a bang. "You are a most incorrigible girl, dead to all the kindness and noble feelings that adorn the character of a woman."

The guard led her away.

There was a small barred window in her room looking out over the Castle courtyard. From it she could see the goings and comings of those who, unlike herself, were still free to walk beneath the open sky. Presently a carriage drove up and stopped just beneath her window. Two soldiers and a man in workman's clothes stepped out. It was John Fleming, the White Bull Tavern hostler. The soldiers turned him over to Tower Keeper Hanlon and drove off. So they had him too! She longed to call down a comforting word.

A few minutes later Hanlon brought the new prisoner up the stairs and shut him in the room next to hers. Through the thin partition she could hear him walking back and forth, moaning and muttering to himself. She coughed several times, so he might guess that a friend was nearby and would have told him who she was, had he asked.

The next morning Hanlon barged into her room. "Come with me. I want to give you some fresh air." There was a smug gleam in his eyes.

He took her into an inner courtyard. Another prisoner was there, too, a young woman with saucy eyes, red-painted lips and a flirtatious manner.

"Good morning, Mr. Hanlon," she said sweetly, putting her hand on his arm.

He shook her off with a playful pinch. "I want both of you to circle the courtyard slowly and come back here to me."

"And why should I parade myself for your pleasure? Anne demanded.

He scowled. "You'll do as you're told."

Her fellow prisoner folded her arm in Anne's and led her off.

"You haven't been caught before, have you?" she asked. "If you had, you'd know that men are all alike, and if you speak pleasant to them, things go a great deal easier. Take a lesson from me. . . ."

Anne was not listening to her chatter. She had just spied Major Sirr standing at a window not twenty feet away, and with him, John Fleming, the simple hostler whom she had spent several hours of the night pitying.

"What's the matter with you?" demanded her companion. "You look as though you had come across the wee people carrying a corpse on a dark night with the banshee wailing."

"It's nothing." They were passing the stable, and she pointed to a horse standing in a stall. "Oh, look! Isn't he a beauty!" She darted into the stable as though she just had to examine the horses's fine points.

Hanlon was on her heels. "What do you think you are doing?"

"I think I have been sufficiently viewed," Anne said sarcastically. Without waiting for his answer, she walked away, back to the courtyard entrance.

"Let her go," she heard her companion say in silky tones.

A woman came out of the Tower as she reached it, a timid-looking creature with drab hair and frightened pale blue eyes.

"Have you seen my husband, Mr. Hanlon?" she asked Anne.

"I have. He's over by the stable."

His wife spied him just as the bold female prisoner placed her arms around his neck.

"Hanlon, please come here!" she called.

Her husband disengaged himself and sauntered across the yard. "What do you want?" His voice was as insolent with her as with his prisoners.

"For your own sake, Hanlon," she pleaded, "be more discreet."

"I'll teach you to mind your own business," he growled, giving his wife a blow which knocked her to the ground.

Though it was none of her business either, Anne helped her to her feet.

"You are a greater ruffian than I thought—to hit a woman and that your own wife!" she exploded.

He looked at her with fury. "If I had my way, I'd give you a whipping you'd never forget, you meddling wench!" he hissed.

"My child, you are in enough trouble as it is, without landing in more for my sake," Mrs. Hanlon said, brushing the dirt from her clothes.

A guard came up to them. "Come with me, Anne Devlin, There's someone wants to see you."

She half suspected who that someone would be and was not surprised to be pushed into a room with John Fleming.

"Good day, Anne," he said.

She did not answer.

Major Sirr walked in. "Do you know this young man, Anne?"

"I do not," she snapped.

"Why, Anne." Fleming smiled sheepishly at her. "You know me very well. You know I was deeply engaged in the conspiracy, though I swear it was against my wishes. Only to keep my employment, which I needed badly, I pretended to Mrs. Dillon and the others that I was one with them. Since it is over, I have done what I have to do."

"There's an honest young man." The major slapped him on the back. "My poor boy, the anxiety, the sleepless nights you have gone through . . . No wonder the girl didn't know you at first."

"You see I have done the right thing, Anne, and you should too," the hostler said eagerly. "Major Sirr says so, and you can see what a fine gentleman he is. Not like those common riffraff that used to swagger into the White Bull like they was cocks of the roost . . ."

He got no further. Anne had hold of his cravat and was twisting it.

"You wretch," she cried out. "You want to swear away my life but I will have yours first."

She tightened her hold. His face grew red, he choked and sputtered, and yet he did not try to defend himself. His hands dangled limply at his side.

"Help!" yelled Major Sirr hysterically. He ran over to a bell and yanked on it. "Fleming! Do something! Stop her!"

Several guards dashed in. Anne was still clutching Fleming's neckpiece, shaking him back and forth like a rat. Sirr looked apoplectic.

"Take her away," he screamed. "Search her. See if she has a knife"

The humor of the situation suddenly struck her. So this was the great Dublin chief of police who had kept the whole town cowering in terror! Why he was frightened out of his wits by a woman not half his size, at least in girth. She let go of Fleming and, without a backward glance, walked out the door. The guards followed her.

Punishment came swiftly. She was put in a narrow and sweltering closet barely long enough to lie down in, with no windows and little air. For a week she saw no one but the guard who brought her a daily ration of bread and water. Then Dr. Trevor came to see her.

"I'm sorry to see you here, Anne. You must have been a very bad girl."

"No, I wasn't," she said sullenly. Then she realized this was the man to whom she had confided her anxiety about Jimmy. "Forgive me, your Honor. I didn't recognize you. My little brother—is he better yet?"

"Why, Anne," he said with an injured air, "you should know I can do nothing for you or your kin, unless you behave better than you have. Now if you will tell me the names of the conspirators, I will show myself your friend."

She stared at him, suddenly comprehending. "Why, you have done nothing for Jimmy, nothing! You are no better than the others."

The next day she was taken to Kilmainham gaol, of which Dr. Edward Trevor, former apothecary's apprentice, was deputy governor.

14

Death of a Martyr

The new Kilmainham gaol had been built in the early 1790's as protection against the dangerous ideas of freedom and independence engendered by the American and French Revolutions. Carved in stone within the arch over the great iron door were five entwined serpents.

"The serpents represent the demons of crime," the guard who accompanied Anne to the gaol explained.

"And which of those serpents represents the crime of patriotism?" she demanded.

The door closed behind her. The guard turned her over to a record keeper.

"Your name?"

"Anne Devlin."

With a flourish, he wrote it in a great book.

"You are number ninety-eight," he said. "When anyone calls 'ninety-eight,' you are to answer.

She reflected that if she had to be a number instead of a person, she was glad hers matched the Rebellion of '98.

Had she been permitted to look over the record keeper's

shoulder, she would have seen that her sisters, Julie and
Mary, admitted four days before, were listed as numbers
ninety-two and ninety-three, and that Robert Emmet (number ninety) had been in Kilmainham even before them.
Had she been allowed to wait an hour or so, she would have
seen her parents brought in—and with them, Jimmy—in-
scribed in the book with numbers ninety-nine and one
hundred.

Briefly they left her in a small room adjoining the record
keeper's office. A woman whom she recognized as the wife
of one of the rebels was seated on a bench. When their turnkey was looking the other way, she whispered to Anne that
she was being released.

"Send word to Mrs. Dillon at the White Bull that John
Fleming has turned informer and that she and her husband
should flee," Anne said softly.

A turnkey took her down a long gloomy corridor lined with
cells. With a large key from the key ring at his waist, he
opened one of them and ordered her inside. She heard the
clanging of the door as he closed and locked it after her.
That clanging of prison doors was to be the most familiar
sound in her new life.

Her cell was about seven feet long and five feet wide. The
walls, ceiling and floor were stone. It was empty except for
some straw in the corner, which served as her bed. The one
window was small, dirty, barred, and too high for her to
reach. The iron door had a small sliding window where
gaoler or turnkey could spy on her, if they so chose. There
was a cleft in the wall next to the door where, beyond an iron
grating, a lantern could be placed from the outside.

She explored each of the walls in turn, hoping to find she
knew not what. On one of them was scratched " '98," and

K

after it "Sean M——" What instrument had this forgotten hero used to chisel the record of his presence? Why had he not finished the writing of his name? The obvious answer occurred to her and she shuddered.

A slovenly attendant brought her dinner—boiled beef, boiled cabbage and boiled potatoes. The portions were minute, the beef rancid, the cabbage sour, but she ate ravenously. It was her first solid food since her arrest. When the attendant returned for her plate, a medium-sized pleasant-faced man dressed in a blue uniform accompanied him.

"I am George Dunn, gaoler of the state prisoners, first and second class," he said aimably. "I thought you would want to know our rules and regulations. State prisoners are persons accused of conspiracy against the Crown. By a law passed through the Irish Parliament, they are favored with more substantial rations than the felons, or common criminals. First-class state prisoners are members of the gentry and are treated accordingly. Their apartments are more spacious than yours and are furnished with chairs, table, feather bed, linen sheets, wool blankets, fireplace and fuel. They have a wide assortment of foods and are permitted to have their families stay with them.

"Your own apartment is plain, since you have been classified as a second-class prisoner, but you will find us fair and just. Unless you are disobedient or impertinent, you will have regular exercise periods. By order of the deputy governor, you are housed in the male section of the gaol and not with the females. This should cause you no inconvenience since our turnkeys are instructed to keep a close watch on you during those periods when the cell doors are left open and when the prisoners can intermingle. Have you any questions?"

She pleaded with him to give her news of her family, but muttering something about that being out of his province, the gaoler departed.

He returned a little later accompanied by a tall, slender woman with blond hair and brown eyes. Although she must have been in her thirties, she was still attractive.

"My wife," Dunn explained. "She's brought you some woman's things."

The small package which Mrs. Dunn handed Anne contained a fresh chemise, a comb, a few pins for her hair, a towel. "I'm grateful to you, ma'am," Anne said.

"It's a disgrace that you should be kept among these men without a woman near you." Mrs. Dunn spoke indignantly in a voice that revealed her English origin. "What was Edward Trevor thinking of?"

"That's enough, Helen," her husband told her quickly. "You'd better go now."

Dr. Trevor showed up in person later in the day.

"What a pity!" he said, shaking his head. "If you had only talked, Anne, you would now be free."

"Save your pity for those who must live their lives with the shame of having talked too much," she retorted.

In a few days her prison life had settled down to a routine. She received two meals a day, bread and milk in the morning and a hot meal, which was seldom even warm, in the afternoon. Her cell door was opened for a morning and afternoon period but she rarely left it, knowing that the turnkeys would be watching her, not for her protection but to see if she recognized any of the other prisoners. However some had already recognized her, and when they passed her cell, they would, if they could do so undetected, whisper news

of what was happening elsewhere in the gaol, or even beyond its confines.

"I was brought in at the same time as your sisters," one
of them told her. "I was struck with their gentle and modest
demeanor and shocked that they must undergo the rigors of
· prison life."

In the same way she learned that her brother Jimmy had
recovered his health and was kept in a cell with her father.
Word came to her, too, that Hanlon, the brutish tower keeper
at the Castle, had ben shot and killed when attempting to
arrest the carpenter, Henry Howley.

Such scraps of miscellaneous information were supple-
mented by Dr. Trevor, who came regularly to report some
new arrest or execution, seeming to take great pleasure in
the recital. She came to dread the appearance of this peculiar individual whom at first sight she had thought handsome
and kind. Once, when the turnkey opened the door for him,
she snapped, "I suppose you have come to tell me of some
other unfortunate who has lost his head at your hands."

"You do me an injustice, Anne," he said suavely. "Your
apartment is very narrow. Would you not like some fresh
air?"

She said, almost repenting her outburst, that she would
like it very much.

The turnkey took her to a bare inner courtyard divided
by a fence which separated the men's section from the
women's. Watch in hand, the turnkey stood at a gate in that
fence, and at a certain moment opened it and told her to pass
through. She did so—and saw Robert Emmet standing there,
holding a ball and racket. He turned his head and their eyes
met.

At the sight of him, she felt her head whirling dizzily; she wanted to sink into the ground. Somehow she managed to scowl a warning of silence to him.

He raised his racket, tossed the ball and struck it. It fell near where she was standing. He came over and stooped down to pick it up. As he did so, he gave her his familiar half-smile and murmured, "Anne, dear, confess what you know of me and obtain your own and your family's release."

She walked past him without a sign of recognition. He threw his ball again, went after it, and met her midway as she turned back. She pretended to limp, bent down, took off a shoe and shook some imaginary gravel from it.

"I thought you would be the last man in the world to encourage me to become an informer."

"I don't mean that," he said softly. "Tell of no one but me. I am a dead man, although I am here."

At a grated window above her, she caught a glimpse of Dr. Trevor standing with several other gentlemen. The sight confirmed her suspicions.

Again she and Mr. Emmet passed each other as strangers.

They met a third time, and she reached down to pull up one of her stockings, the only device she could think of.

"There is a watch on the windows," she warned him.

"There will be enough to swear against me, Anne," he said anxiously. I cannot die easy while you and your family are in danger because of me."

"I will not swear one word."

They continued to walk back and forth a little while longer, taking no apparent notice of each other. Then the turnkey called her to come inside.

Dr. Trevor arrived at her cell almost immediately.

"So? You decided to be clever and pretend not to recognize Robert Emmet," he exploded angrily.

"Who?" she asked.

"You don't fool any of us, Anne Devlin. There is no use pretending you are innocent."

"The gentlemen who were with you at the window are perhaps annoyed with you for bringing them from the Castle for nothing?" she demanded guilelessly. "What a shame!"

Her dart struck home. "You rebelly wench!" he shouted. "I have seen but one woman hanged, yet I swear I would go any distance to see you hanged. I would feel a pleasure in pulling the rope."

It was almost a relief to have him discard his mask of pretended friendship.

For her "impertinence," Trevor sent her for three days' solitary confinement in the dungeon. This was a damp and gloomy cell below ground level. The only light was from an opening into the courtyard no more than the size of a brick; her only sustenance was bread and water—the rations of the felons. The advantage was that during her stay she did not once see Dr. Trevor.

On September 2, the first day she was returned to the state prisoners' corridor, he was back again to taunt her with more executions:

"Edward Kearney—you know him well, Anne. He was captured on the night of July 23, bearing arms. I thought you would like to know his last words. 'This is a bad business, boys,' he told the crowd standing before his gallows. 'I advise you to have nothing more to do with it.' "

"You are lying!" Anne spat at him.

"I assure you I speak the truth. Tomorrow, it will be the turn of two other friends—Thomas Roche and Owen Kirwan."

"I know not those poor men," she said.

"What thoughts are running through their heads now?" he went on ruthlessly. "Do you really think they are congratulating themselves for following a leader who took advantage of them for the sake of his own ambition?"

She clenched her teeth and said nothing.

"Why are you so blind, Anne?" Once more, as he invariably did, he urged her to come out and tell all she knew.

"A black curse on you," she said wearily—a remark that brought her several more days in solitary confinement.

She was back in her own cell on September 20, when he came again. His swarthy face was beaming with such jubilation that she knew she must be ready for anything.

"I wanted you to be the first to know, Anne. His trial was held yesterday. It lasted twelve hours without a break and no one can say it was not fair, but he called not a single witness in his defense. You can guess for yourself the decision of the judge. Tomorrow he will hang, then be beheaded."

"I don't know whom you are talking about."

"Your darling, Robert Emmet, of course. But then he is everyone's darling, is he not? Or didn't you know of the very highly placed young lady whose letters were found on his person when he was arrested? I should not say anything about that, I suppose, for the last thing in the world I would want is to grieve you. They say her father was so angry that he drove her from his house forever. A shame we don't have his letters to her, but it seems her sister burned them before Major Sirr had a chance to stop her."

If she could only scratch the eyes out of this malicious fiend! If she could only die herself, as Robert Emmet was going to. Poor Sarah Curran—what she must be suffering! Brave Amelia Curran, whose quick thinking had kept the revelations of Robert Emmet's letters from a hostile world. With all the terrible emotions Dr. Trevor's words had caused, she managed to look at him stonily as though she did not know what he was talking about.

With exquisite cruelty, Trevor had one more drama in store for her.

Early the next morning, George Dunn, the gaoler, opened her cell. "Prepare yourself, Anne. We are going for an outing."

She followed him down the corridor and out of the gaol. A coach was waiting.

"Get in, Anne."

Two soldiers guarded her, one on each side, with drawn bayonets. Dunn, holding a brace of pistols, stepped up with the driver. They drove off in the direction of the Castle, but came to a halt at beautiful St. Catherine's Church on Thomas Street—not far from Mr. Emmet's depot.

In front of the church was erected a rude gallows. Beneath it, several dogs and pigs were lapping up the blood which had formed in little pools between the paving stones, the blood of the man of whom Big Art had once said, "His heart is aflame with love of Ireland and his spirit afire to set her free."

She closed her eyes and tried to pray but the words would not come.

15

Kitty, The Goose

On the theory that the sight of the gallows which had taken Robert Emmet's life would weaken her morale, Anne was brought directly to the Castle for a second examination by Secretaries Marsden and Wickham. They read her a list of names and asked if any of those mentioned had ever come to Butterfield Lane.

"If they did, it was not likely they would allow a strange servant maid to know their secrets," she said.

"You still insist you were only a servant?"

"I was."

"And since when does a servant dare say to her master, 'Bad welcome to you. . . .'" Secretary Wickham continued, quoting the other remarks she had made to Robert Emmet and his men the night of July 23.

She remained silent, trying her utmost to conceal her consternation.

"You see, Anne, there is little we do not know about you. There are, for instance, your three outlaw cousins. You are fond of them, are you not? Would you not like to be responsible for their protection?"

"They would not care to be protected through the blood of their comrades," she replied.

They had her taken back to Kilmainham and the mercies of Dr. Trevor, the deputy governor. He promptly had her thrown in the dungeon for her "recalcitrance." She spent a week in solitary confinement; the guard tossed her bread to her as though she were a dog. Then she was brought back to her old cell.

"Well, have you learned your lesson, Anne?" Dr. Trevor demanded on his next visit.

"You are a blackguard!" she screamed at him, her hair matted and her eyes wild.

News came to her as before, through the prison underground. Nicholas Stafford, the baker, and Michael Quigley, the bricklayer, had both been arrested. Henry Howley, the carpenter, had been executed for the "murder" of Tower Keeper Hanlon. The gallant Thomas Russell gave his life for his country on October 21, at Downpatrick gaol. He had been in the North at the time of the uprising, but had risked returning to Dublin to organize a plot to effect Robert Emmet's escape. An informer had recognized him and he was arrested. He gave the Castle no information but what they knew already. "As many tears are being shed for Robert Emmet as would bathe him," he said in his examination.

The Lord Lieutenant issued a proclamation offering five hundred pounds for information leading to the arrest of Michael Dwyer. When no one came to claim it, all of Dwyer's family as well as many of his neighbors were arrested. The men were loaded on prison ships. The women, one after another, were brought to Kilmainham. Among them were Kathy and Dwyer's other sisters. (Kathy's husband John

O'Neil had already been arrested.) Anne was naturally not allowed to see them.

Not long afterward, Dr. Trevor came to announce: "Michael Dwyer and your other cousins have all been arrested."

Anne took a deep breath. "My father once had a bald horse with a wicked disposition," she said. "Whenever he was mischief bent, he would get a sly side look in his eyes and there would appear a red shade over them—just as yours do when you come here to tell me some horrible story, Dr. Trevor."

The turnkey, standing behind him, snickered.

"I'll teach you to laugh at the wench's insolence!" Trevor roared, striking him across the face.

Winter had arrived in full force, bringing its added load of misery to the prisoners. The small brazier at the end of the corridor did not extend its warmth to Anne's "apartment." Cold, confinement and inadequate food had taken their toll. She had lost weight; her bones and muscles ached constantly.

One stormy night as she lay shivering under her thin blanket, she heard her cell door open.

"It is I—Helen Dunn," said a woman's voice. "Follow me, Anne. I'm bringing you to my quarters."

The gaoler's wife took her down a hallway, up a flight of stairs, and through a back door which opened into a pleasant kitchen where a warm fire was burning in the fireplace. Anne looked at it yearningly.

"Warm yourself, Anne," her hostess said. She was dressed simply in a dark blue gown with a white fichu, her blond hair coiffed in a neat coil, but the finest lady in the land could not have been more gracious. She pulled a chair near the fire, bade Anne sit down, then poured her a bowl of hot broth. "Drink this. It will do you good."

"And if your husband should be finding me here?" Anne asked.

"He won't. He is at the tavern—where he goes every night to forget the man he has become."

Mrs. Dunn did not explain this odd statement, nor did Anne venture to question her. She stayed about an hour, then the gaoler's wife escorted her back. After the brief interlude, her cell seemed doubly cheerless.

All that bitter winter, Mrs. Dunn came to get her several times a week, feeding her nourishing meals, supplying her with warm water to bathe and to wash her prison-stained clothes. Without her kindness, it seemed to Anne she could not have survived.

"Why does Dr. Trevor so persecute me?" Anne asked her once.

"You must understand that he is an ambitious man, Anne." Mrs. Dunn paused. "I know him well. His official duties are to see that the gaol is properly maintained, but no, he must take on himself to try to get confessions where the Castle has failed—as if that would put a feather in his cap. He has his own staff of informers . . ." She stopped, as though afraid of saying too much.

"I still do not see why I should be given the benefit of so much of his attention," Anne puzzled.

"You are a woman," Mrs. Dunn said shortly. "He cannot stand to see any woman defy him."

In time, Mrs. Dunn let her maid in on their secret. She was a shy, friendly girl, who went out of her way to make Anne comfortable. Once Mrs. Dunn brought Anne up on a Sunday afternoon for tea, having first made certain that Dr.

Trevor had completed his rounds and departed. Anne asked if she could help the maid prepare dinner, saying what a great treat it would be after her long enforced idleness. Mrs. Dunn agreed, and then left on some errand.

The maid and Anne were in the kitchen laughing and chatting, when the door burst open and Dr. Trevor stormed in. The maid fled in terror.

"So, Anne Devlin! I was told I would find you here," he cried out triumphantly, seizing her by the shoulders. "I see you still have people to befriend you in spite of my orders. There's going to be an end to such liberties."

Her first thought was for Mrs. Dunn. "Your Honor, I beg you to blame no one but myself for my presence here," she pleaded, resolving not to answer him back no matter what he said.

"I am happy to tell you that a court-martial at the Castle has passed sentence on you," he snarled. "You will be hanged within five days."

"On what charge?" she asked, half believing him.

"As a warning to all women not to keep a secret," he chortled.

Her good resolution was forgotten: "You had better laugh at your own jokes for no one else will."

He slapped her. "As a matter of fact, hanging is much too good for you. You will be put among the women felons, under the care of one who will soon murder you. Get back to your cell and prepare yourself."

He marched out.

When Mrs. Dunn returned, Anne told her tearfully what had happened. "I fear I have brought you trouble."

"It's on yourself you have brought trouble," said Mrs.

Dunn, imitating Anne's Irish speech. "What punishment has he thought up now?"

Anne shrugged. "I'm to be put with the women felons. At least I shall have other women to talk with. But what did he mean when he said he would put me in the care of one who would murder me?"

Mrs. Dunn bit her lip. "Kitty, the Goose," she said.

The "women felons" were kept on the opposite side of the gaol from the state prisoners. The luxury of private cells was not for them; they were all herded together in one barred room. Their crimes ranged from picking pockets to the most heinous of foul deeds. One had cut the throat of her own infant. Another had lured a gentleman who had "a drop too much taken" down a dark alley, where her companions were waiting to murder and rob him. The ancient crones in rags and the young women in remnants of cheap finery had in common a background of abysmal poverty where vice was both an escape and a necessity for survival.

When the guard thrust Anne unceremoniously in their midst, she was greeted with a storm of abuse. What was she doing there with her airs of a gentlewoman? Had she come, in her fine clothes, to spy on them? Anne was wearing a plain gray gown, which regulations required be issued to female state prisoners when their own was beyond repair. Did she think herself better than they? She would soon find out that here they were all cut from the same cloth.

"Do not hate me," Anne pleaded desperately. "I, like yourselves, am the victim of oppression."

Her words only evoked foul curses. Inwardly she prayed that God grant her compassion for these beings who seemed bereft of all human kindness and decency.

Among them was one who dominated the others by the right of physical strength and wickedness. This was an enormous woman, weighing at least three hundred pounds, with coarse, black matted hair and thick eyebrows above a crafty face. Kitty, the Goose, owed her nickname to her predilection of stealing geese and other fowl from the Dublin markets, though she often boasted of more sinister crimes. From dawn until dusk, she strode around their cell, making her presence felt, shouting, singing bawdy songs, cursing, bragging. She told the other women what to do, and, for a whim, struck them or yanked them by the hair. When it seized her fancy, she stole their meager bread rations, daring them to do anything about it. The guards, who were convicts themselves, looked on in amusement.

Anne was soon singled out for Kitty's special persecution. On more than one occasion she woke in the night to see that evil face hanging over her. "I'm going to twist the life out of that white neck, my little goose." Anne would jump up screaming, but her cries brought only smothered oaths from those whose slumber she had interrupted.

Day in and day out, she lived a nightmare. The stiffness in her body increased. Her legs became inflamed and swollen. "Get me a doctor," she begged the guard one morning, when she was suffering more than she could bear.

"Kitty will soon free you from pain," he said with a short laugh.

That day they were ordered out in the exercise yard. The sky above the prison walls was softly blue with foamy clouds moving lazily across it, and the air was warm and sweet. In the close and fetid atmosphere of the prison, Anne had almost forgotten that spring was under way. A few blades of grass had pushed their way bravely through a crack in the stone pavement. How good it was to see something green and growing! As she stooped to look at it more closely she saw a long and shiny butcher's knife lying on the ground a few feet away.

She started to pick it up and give it to the guards for safekeeping, but Kitty was ahead of her. With a quick movement she grabbed it, and brandishing it high, laughed like a maniac.

"Take it away from her, you idiots!" Anne called to the guards. "She might harm someone."

"Now we'll have a bit of fun," one guard said to his mate.

The next instant Kitty had whirled on Anne. "You think I'd harm someone? Well so I might, my little chicken."

Holding the knife poised, she advanced step by step, as Anne retreated. "Kitty, you'll only get yourself in trouble," she said, trying to reason with her. "Do be thinking what you're doing, Kitty, or they'll punish you more than they've done already."

"What do I care what they do to me, the scum? I'm going to get you first!" she shouted.

Anne felt her back touch the wall; she had retreated as far as she could. Then Kitty was upon her, her eyes insane and her mouth foaming, pressing her throat with one hand and, with the other, bringing the knife slowly closer. Anne screamed, again and again.

Suddenly the "woman felons," those pitiful derelicts she had thought devoid of all human feeling, were swarming over Kitty, pulling her away from Anne, striking her wrist till she dropped the knife, and then clinging onto her arms and legs until other guards came running, "What's going on here?"

Someone snapped irons on Kitty and led her away. Anne

collapsed to the ground. She looked up to see George Dunn, whose pleasant face had convinced many rebel prisoners he was on their side. Behind him was Helen Dunn.

"Anne, are you all right? We heard your screams even from our own quarters."

"I'm not hurt." She got to her feet. "Just frightened out of my senses."

"I'm taking her back with me, George," Mrs. Dunn told her husband.

"You can't do that, ma'am. She's in our charge," answered the guard who had wanted to have "a bit of fun."

"Not any more," she told him icily.

The Dunn kitchen was warm, cozy and clean. Mrs. Dunn sent her husband out while she bathed Anne's swollen face and limbs.

"You shouldn't," sobbed Anne. "I'm more nuisance than I'm worth."

"Don't fret about that."

She gave her a clean apron and blouse to put on and served her some hot tea. Anne was sitting up, drinking it, when Dr. Trevor barged in, the two guards from the women felon's quarters behind him.

"So no matter where one puts you, you always get out!"

"How can you speak like that, Edward?" Mrs. Dunn interposed. "Don't you see she is sick?"

"She's going to be sicker when I am through with her." He motioned to the guards. "Take her back."

Anne felt herself trembling uncontrollably. "You would not be returning me to Kitty, the Goose, who tried to murder me?"

"I am." He smiled maliciously.

"No! No!" she cried out, weeping hysterically. Sinking to

her knees she grabbed hold of his coat tails. "I beg of you, your Honor, kill me if you will, but don't make me go back to the women felons." It was the only time in her life when Trevor saw her thus.

He pulled himself away coldly. "I assure you, Anne Devlin, that if you went on your head after being on your knees, it would not make an iota of difference to me."

"The lass needs a doctor, not more punishment, Trevor," said George Dunn, who had come in unobserved.

The deputy governor stared at him in astonishment. "And since when do you tell me my job, Dunn?"

"I would not do that, sir, but I would like to be reminding you that should she die of unnatural causes, an investigation would be an unpleasant thing for all of us." The words were spoken mildly, but even in her disordered state, Anne grasped that the gaoler was performing perhaps the most courageous act of his life.

Dr. Trevor's face went dark red. "All right, all right," he growled. "Do what you like with her. I wash my hands of the whole affair." He stalked out, followed by the guards.

Mrs. Dunn flung her arms around her husband. "I'm proud of you, George."

He released himself, shaking his head. "She should never have said it."

"Said what?"

"She should never have compared Trevor to her father's old bald horse. The Castle found out and they are still laughing. That's one thing he'll never forgive."

Suddenly he chuckled. "Trevor, the old bald horse," he chanted, slapping his knee with his hand. "Trevor, the old bald horse. That's a good one!"

16

The Old Gaol

"Congratulations, Anne Devlin. Your mother and sisters have been set free."

She was back in her old cell. The joyous news, called through the grating by her door, made her own sufferings seem unimportant.

Her fellow inhabitants of the state prisoner corridor, second class, greeted her like a sister returned from America. They were mostly young men of the working class who had been rounded up on suspicion with no definite charge against them. More frequently than before, they found ways of passing along to Anne the news they picked up in the exercise yard or through outside visitors.

Thus she learned that her brother John, who had not been at Kilmainham but held in the Ship Street guardhouse, was also free. John Mahon and Thomas Wilde, two of Mr. Emmet's closest companions, had actually escaped the claws of the Castle and were on their way to America. Few others were as fortunate.

Michael Dwyer, Big Art, Hugh Vesty Byrne were all at

Kilmainham, but it was not true, as Trevor had said, that they were captured. They had surrendered, to stop the persecution of their families and neighbors, and that on their own terms: that all those arrested on their account should be set free; and that they be given passage to the United States.

When were they leaving? Her informants could not tell her. It was maddening to know that they were so near and that she had no more chance of seeing them than had they remained in the Vale of Imaal.

The anniversary of her first year at Kilmainham was marked only by a visit from Dr. Trevor.

"Well, Anne, how are you feeling?" he asked her benignly.

She had been rubbing her legs, trying to relieve the swelling. "I am twelve months under your care and growing worse every day," she snapped.

"If you would but take my advice, you would soon grow better."

"If it be your advice, I'll never obey one word of it."

Every time a new arrest was made, he appeared, cajoling, threatening, bullying her to testify against the prisoner.

"You need only say a few words, Anne. We naturally have proof of guilt already."

It did not take much intelligence to see that if they had proof of guilt, they would not need her testimony. "Haven't you yet learned you are wasting your time?"

When Dr. Trevor goaded her too far, she screamed insults at him, calling him the vilest names she could invent. It gave her a peculiar satisfaction to do so, but the result was always punishment. She was sent again and again to the dungeon and solitary confinement, or to the "Stag's Hall" where Trevor kept his informers. She was even returned to the women felons, but since Kitty, the Goose, had been taken away she no longer minded.

She was not the only person victimized by Dr. Edward Trevor. There were complaints about his conduct even among the first-class state prisoners. Two of them, Barrister St. John Mason, a cousin of Robert Emmet's; and a wealthy gentleman named Edward Kennedy, held because he was a half brother of Miles Byrnes, prepared a petition to the Lord Lieutenant, citing a long list of grievances. "His treatment of all," it read in part, "but particularly of one unfortunate state prisoner (a female) is shocking to humanity and and exceeds all credibility."

In time three judges from the Castle came to Kilmainham to make an inquiry. A few minor improvements resulted, but the judges never did bother to see the "unfortunate state prisoner (a female)," which of course referred to Anne Devlin.

She had received no medical treatment for her strange malady, which had worsened. Walking had become increasingly painful. Her eyesight was affected; there were times when she could hardly see at all. And her second winter in prison was under way.

One morning in early December of 1804, George Dunn came for her with another guard. "You are to come with us, Anne. Bring your bedding."

She groaned with the effort of rising. "Where to now, George?"

"You'll find out soon enough."

She limped between the two men as far as the small office where she had waited on first entering the gaol. A boy was sitting on a bench all alone. Her sight, as usual, was blurred. It did not occur to her that she might know him.

"Anne! Anne!" He came rushing over to her and threw his arms around her neck. "Don't you know me?"

"Jimmy!" Incredulously. she pressed him to her. He was so thin that his ribs almost protruded beyond his flesh. Smallpox had left its scars on his sweet face. He had grown hardly at all since last she had seen him. But he had survived! That in itself was miraculous.

"I've missed you, Anne!" he said.

He was flushed, unnaturally so. She put her hand to his forehead.

"You have a fever, Jimmy."

" 'Tis nothing, Anne. Are they setting us free?"

"I trust so."

"Don't be putting hopes in the boy's head," growled George Dunn, picking up her bedding.

They went outside, past the great gate. An icy blast pierced Anne's thin clothing.

"We can't take my brother into this weather," she shrieked at George above the wind.

"I have my orders, Anne."

They cut across the fields, Anne struggling to make her crippled limbs do her bidding and trying at the same time to shield Jimmy. Presently a gloomy ruin loomed ahead of them. It was the Old Gaol. After the new Kilmainham had been built, it had been abandoned. Now Dr. Trevor had found it could be used after all.

Several soldiers with bayonets were on guard at the gate. A turnkey opened the rusty iron door to let them in. He was a short little man, round as a ball and bald as a cockroach.

"Two new ones," he chuckled. "That's good. Three old ones went out this morning with black cloth over their faces. This is one hotel that will never get full."

He called a guard, a ferocious-looking fellow with a black mustache and a long scar across the side of his face. "This attendant will escort you to your apartment." He laughed as though he had made a wicked jest.

"I'm sorry, Anne," said George Dunn, looking uncomfortable. He handed her the bedding and left.

The guard took them up a flight of stone steps and unlatched a door at the top. It was not even locked—as though whoever was inside would not bother to try an escape.

"Go right in, miss," the guard told her, leering. "If you want privacy, there are some vacant apartments on the far side. You can take your pick." With that, he walked off rapidly.

She understood his haste as she entered and the foul air of pestilence struck her nostrils. She was in a large hall, with walls chipped and crumbling and ceiling dripping. A fire was burning in a battered stove, filling the room with smoke which set Anne and her brother to coughing. Around it huddled a group of phantoms, hardly human, half clothed, dirty, emaciated, so alike in their wretchedness it was difficult to tell whether they were male or female. Others lay on the floor, moaning and whimpering.

Anne had heard a rumor that a fever epidemic had broken out among the felons and that the sick were being removed. She had thought it was to a hospital.

"Anne, are we going to stay here?" little Jimmy asked, his voice filled with horror.

"No, darling, of course not, except perhaps for a little while."

She tightened her hold on him and pulled him past the poor spectral creatures around them. This then was Dr. Trevor's last revenge—to send her and her brother to this place of the living dead. Once again, as in the past, the thought of him stiffened her will to survive.

There were, as the guard had said, several cells at the far end of the hall. They were open, their doors hanging useless on their hinges. Distant from the one source of heat, the other inmates avoided them. The windowpanes were broken; there were only iron gratings to keep out wind and rain. But the air, though cold, was at least free from contagion. Anne selected the one that seemed least filthy and least damp; there was in truth little choice.

"You must do everything I tell you so you will get well," she said, kneeling down by her brother.

"Yes, Anne." He looked around critically. "It could not be much worse, could it?"

"No, it couldn't." She smiled sadly at him. "Shall we try to make the best of what we cannot help?"

"I have learned to do so since last I saw you."

She realized with a pang that he had left his childhood far behind him.

Unrolling her blanket, she spread it on the floor. "Lie down now."

As she covered him, he looked up at her thoughtfully. "After Mother and Mary and Julie left, they let me stay with Father. He is all alone now. Do you think we will ever be together again?"

"I'm sure we will." She tried to make her words convincing but she could tell he was not fooled.

By evening he was delirious.

She ran through the inferno of the dying, out the door and up and down the halls until she found the lair of her guard, who was playing cards and drinking ale with some cronies. She did not need to be told that they were criminals of the lowest sort, who had taken this dangerous assignment as preferable to a hanging.

"I do not have prison fever nor does my brother," she cried, to forestall being thrown out, "but he will get pneumonia if he is not kept warm."

Putting aside her pride like a garment of no value, she pleaded with them for clean straw, another blanket, a pail of fresh water. When they looked at her as if she were daft, she remembered the lessons of the female prisoner in the Castle yard and smiled at them sweetly—as she had done to no man since her arrest. She begged other necessities from the round little turnkey, and to some degree met with success.

The next days—when she wasn't asking favors—she sat beside her brother, talking to him comfortingly, holding a damp rag to his forehead. Finally one afternoon, he opened his eyes and smiled wanly.

"I'm hungry, Anne."

It was Christmas Eve. She raced to the turnkey.

"I must get some solid food for my brother." All they doled out at the Old Gaol was bread and sometimes cold potatoes. The place did not boast a kitchen.

"You again!" the turnkey grumbled.

"Please! My brother's fever has passed. He will live—if he can eat."

Suddenly he looked very pleased with himself. "Why, yes, ma'am, I can let you have something. A basket was brought to you by Mrs. Dunn's maid." He stepped into his den and brought out a straw basket covered with a white napkin. "I was going to have it sent to you."

She knew he would have done no such thing. Only because she had appeared at the proper moment had the Yuletide

spirit triumphed over greed. Thanking him profusely for his
"generosity," she tore back to her cell with the basket.

"Here, Jimmy. Father Christmas has been here in person
and left us a gift."

She lifted the napkin from the basket and brought out a
roast chicken, a jar of jelly, white bread, butter, cakes and
other delicacies.

"God grant you your dearest wish, Helen Dunn," she
murmured.

That night they had a feast.

Within a couple of weeks, Jimmy seemed completely well.
Since he was not officially a prisoner, the turnkey allowed
him out in the courtyard to play. No objections were raised
either when he asked permission to go up to see his father.
Wistfully, Anne watched him through her bars as he bounded
across the bleak fields lightly as a rabbit.

Whenever the weather permitted, he went regularly to
Kilmainham during the next weeks. One day he returned,
his eyes bright. His mother had visited them while he was
there.

"How is she?" demanded Anne eagerly.

"She is fine," he said. And he went on to say that prison
life had not been good for her. Her hair was white now, like
their father's. She and Mary and Julie were staying in Dublin
with a distant cousin. John was working as a carter to support them, but his health was poor too. He had asked after
Nellie, and his mother had looked unhappy, saying that the
woman who had taken her had been arrested like themselves, and Nellie had been sent to an orphanage. They had
not yet found any trace of her, but Mother had assured him
they would soon do so.

Shortly after that, Jimmy was returned to his father. Anne

knew he would be better off there than in this dreadful den of disease, but she was fearfully lonely without him. As long as he had been around she had, by force of will, pushed aside her own illness. Now she was no longer able to do so. The old aches and pains returned, and she lay on her straw day after day, without the strength to move.

Winter yielded slowly to the blandishments of spring. Late in March, after a few mild days, a blizzard raged. All day, Anne shivered on her thin pallet as the howling wind shot gusts of sleet through her window.

Toward evening, the guard came to her cell, the one with the dark mustache and the long scar who had first escorted her in. He was carrying a large bundle, which he deposited at her side. It was Jimmy—a Jimmy with eyes wide and unseeing, clothes soaked, and with a burning fever.

With a frightened moan, Anne gathered him to her.

The guard, callous to human suffering as he was, looked ashamed. "I had nothing to do with it, ma'am. They walked him all the way in that storm. He has had the prison fever about a week." With something like indignation he added, "They should not have let him walk. 'Twas a brutal thing."

Her brother never fully regained consciousness and died in her arms the next night. The Castle and Dr. Trevor had claimed their first victim from the Devlin family.

17

A True Friend

Shortly after Jimmy's death she was brought back to Kilmainham, by mule cart, for she could not walk.

Dr. Trevor was her first visitor. He pretended to be sympathetic to her plight. "I'll tell you what I'll do, Anne. I'll get you a pair of crutches."

"Keep them for some of your friends," she snapped.

Her loathing for him was so intense she could not bear to look at him.

That night Mrs. Dunn came for her. She had brought her maid, and between them they supported her to the Dunn apartment. A tall, fine-looking gentleman was sitting in the kitchen. Anne started to back out.

"That's all right, Anne," Mrs. Dunn reassured her. "This is Mr. Edward Kennedy, a prisoner like yourself. He asked to see you."

Anne remembered that he was one of those who had sent a petition to the Lord Lieutenant, in which he mentioned her.

"Hello, Anne," he said rising. "We have not met before

though I have heard much about you. You should know that you are famous throughout the prison for your heroism in the face of terrible adversity. Your courage is an inspiration to us all."

"You are very kind, sir." His compliments stunned her but she could not accept them. "In truth I am not at all heroic." She told him how once, in desperation, she had gone on her knees to Dr. Trevor.

"That's only shows you are human, making your courage the more remarkable," he said gently. "The important thing is that, down on your knees or not, you betrayed no one. There are many men, big and strong, who cannot say as much."

The maid helped her to a chair and served her some tea.

"I speak for my fellow prisoners in offering you sympathy for the cruel death of your brother," Mr. Kennedy continued. "We are preparing a new petition for the Lord Lieutenant and we want to state the case in full. Would it be too painful for you to tell me just what happened?"

"I'll try, sir." Blinking back the tears that the thought of Jimmy evoked in her, she described his bitter ordeal.

"I thought so." Kennedy stood up and started pacing the floor. "To his other crimes, Trevor has added the murder of an innocent child. Our petition will go out tomorrow, Anne. I'm not saying anything will come of it. Trevor is necessary to the Castle. They cannot publicly condone his conduct, but they can and do feign blindness. At least, the story will be in the public record. In addition, my fellow prisoner, St. John Mason, more literate than I, is writing his memoirs so that future generations will know the dastardly events that transpired here."

A week after the sending of the petition, Trevor came, bringing a stranger to her cell.

"This is Dr. Vaughan," he said. "I have asked him to look into your case."

She suspected that Vaughan might be another informer, but she was wrong. He was in truth a physician of standing, not an "apothecary's apprentice" like Trevor.

"Your malady is erysipelas," he told her after his examination. "I must tell you frankly that, though it is not uncommon, very little is known about its cause or treatment. I will do for you what I can."

His was the first medical attention she had received since her arrest. He did not succeed in curing her, but his solicitude for her condition did her a world of good.

She was granted at this time the freedom of the women's quarters, a room where the wives of state prisoners and other women congregated during the day. Among them was Michael Dwyer's wife, the former Mary Doyle.

"Michael and I have been destroying ourselves with worry about you," Mary cried out, embracing her warmly. "The first thing Michael did when he was brought here was to ask to see you, not knowing then about Trevor and his rules. Of course permission was denied."

Mary was the mother of three children now, two boys and a small baby girl. She had them with her, and in fact they were all staying with her husband during his confinement. For this devoted wife, prison with her husband was better than the outside world without him.

Though Michael's sisters and parents had been released, the authorities had stalled on their promise to send him to the United States. Michael had made several vigorous protests about this lack of faith, but so far all these protests had

resulted in were a few visits to the dungeon. Big Arthur had
endured the same punishment for his "intractability." Hugh
Vesty was there with them; in spite of what they had endured, all three were in good health and spirits.

The reunion with Mary Doyle Dwyer would have been
altogether joyous had Anne not been so sick and crippled.
But now it seemed that Dr. Trevor, who had been so anxious
to have her hanged, actually wanted her to get well. One
day she was informed that she was to go to Lucan Spa, a
watering spot about seven miles away, to bathe in the min-
eral waters—and that she could take her sister Julie as her
woman companion.

Julie came to the gaol to meet her. She was extremely thin
and pale and poorly dressed, but there was a radiant smile
on her face. "Anne, our darling Anne," she kept repeating
over and over.

A jaunting car—a carriage with facing seats—had been
hired for the excursion. Julie and Anne sat on one side and
opposite them a scowling turnkey armed with two braces of
heavy pistols. His presence effectively kept them from ex-
changing confidences but did not mar Anne's enjoyment of
the drive along the winding river Liffey, the wonder of
being under the open sky once more, or her pleasure at her
sister's company.

There were several more visits to Lucan Spa after that.
Whether from the celebrated waters or merely because of
the change from prison life, she improved enormously. The
swelling went down, her pains diminished, she felt herself
almost a normal human being again.

Abruptly the excursions ceased. She was once more confined to her cell, forbidden the women's quarters.

"Trevor is preparing a defense against the prisoners'

charges of misconduct," one of her cell neighbors explained. "Dr. Vaughan, Lucan Spa, all the rest of it, will be offered as proof that he has more than indulged you."

From the same person she learned that the Dwyer family had left Kilmainham, not for the United States, but on a convict ship headed for Australia. Big Art and Hugh Vesty Byrne had gone with them. She would never see any of them again and she had not been allowed to say good-by. She and her father were the only ones of their family left in Kilmainham, though Little Arthur, poor lad, was still held in Provost prison, in another part of Dublin.

The heat of summer turned to the chill of autumn and then to the cold of winter, her third in prison. The erysipelas returned to plague her. Had not Mrs. Dunn continued to bring her to her apartment, her life would have been too bleak to bear. She knew, as all the prisoners now did, that George Dunn was an informer, that all those whose trust he won by his agreeable manner had their confidences duly repeated to Dr. Trevor. That sad knowledge did not alter her deep gratitude to George Dunn's wife.

Early in 1806, exciting news spread through the prison. William Pitt, the Tory prime minister who had so long been a bitter foe to Irish patriots, had breathed his last. Pitt's successor, Charles James Fox, was a Whig, the more liberal of the two British parties, and leniency could be expected of him.

"London has demanded a list of political prisoners," Anne was informed by one of those prisoners. "Soon it will all be over."

But Dr. Trevor was not going to let her out of his clutches so easily.

Early one dreary February morning, George Dunn ordered her out of her cell and drove her to the Castle. There she was taken to the Tower and left in a small closet without light or heat or fresh air, much like the one where she had been confined in punishment for half-strangling John Fleming more than three years before. The punishment had seemed drastic at the time, though it had been for only a week and she had then been strong and healthy.

As the door closed on her, she was struck with the horrible thought that she would stay here until she died, forgotten by all the world. Soon it will be all over for me, she thought, echoing in despair the words her fellow prisoner had uttered in hope.

Once again it was one of her own sex who brought her comfort.

She had been about a fortnight in this black hole, seeing no one but the sullen guard, when one night her door was opened and a woman entered.

"I am Mrs. Hanlon. You will perhaps not remember me but I saw you when you were here before, Anne Devlin."

The trembling frightened person whose brutal husband, now dead, had knocked her to the ground!

"I remember you well, Mrs. Hanlon."

For a moment she stood looking down at Anne by the light of a lantern in the hall. Then suddenly she knelt at her side, her eyes filled with compassion.

"So this is the work of that monster of Kilmainham. You poor child. If I could only find some way to help you, it would give me such pleasure. But how? Since my husband's death, I hold the title of tower keeper, but it is an empty honor. I am almost as much a prisoner as you, with spies and informers watching my every move."

M

"I assure you, madam, that your sympathy alone means everything," said Anne, choked with emotion.

"You need more than sympathy." Mrs. Hanlon stroked her hair gently. "I will come to you when I can and do for you what is possible. In the meantime I bring you news that will help to drive anguish from your heart. London has received the list of political prisoners at Kilmainham and has ordered the release of all of them. Your father is now a free man."

"You are sure?" Forgetting her pain, Anne sat upright.

"I am sure. Try to be brave a little longer, Anne, dear. I will be back."

When she left, Anne broke down and cried—but for once hers were tears of joy.

Not too long afterward, Mrs. Hanlon paid a second nocturnal visit, bringing more good news. Little Arthur had been released from Provost prison. This was not due to the government amnesty but to the humanity and kindness of a certain Judge Day.

"Judge Day, whoever you may be, God bless you," Anne murmured.

Now her whole family would be waiting for her when she got out. She imagined them as they used to be, not at Rathfarnham, which had never been truly their home, but in their whitewashed thatched cottage in the green fields of county Wicklow. She saw her father, erect and black-bearded and grave; her mother, so wise and generous; gentle Mary and vivacious Julie; the husky, good-natured John, and Little Arthur so eager to explore the world of learning. The babies were there, too, in this daydream, for her mind could not accept the death of Jimmy or the disappearance of little Nellie.

There was an empty room next to her closet. Occasionally the guard opened the door and allowed her in. With tremendous effort, she would crawl around the four sides. Once she managed to reach up and place a few crumbs on the window sill. A covey of starlings darted down and devoured them, noisily and greedily. It seemed to her that she had never seen anything so beautiful as those black birds. But the time came when the effort of crawling was too much for her, and she spent days as well as nights stretched out on her thin pallet.

Mrs. Hanlon came as often as she dared, always bringing fruit or other foods to supplement the inadequate prison fare. On occasion she took Annie's clothes at night and returned with them before dawn, fresh and clean. For those small things that are a necessity for a woman's self-esteem— a brush for her hair, soap and warm water with which to bathe herself—she would be eternally grateful to the tower keeper's widow.

When Anne tried to express her gratitude, she only shook her head. "The one thing that will help you, my child, is to get out of here." They were both aware by now that Dr. Trevor had ordered her placed in the Castle, so he would not have to list her as one of his political prisoners to whom an amnesty was due.

Mrs. Hanlon took it on herself to approach a gentleman she believed had influence in the Castle and ask him to intercede on Anne's behalf. He promised to do so, but weeks passed and nothing happened. The gentleman, it seemed, was more liberal with promises than with actions.

Her next step was a bold one. She sent a letter to Chief Secretary Long, who occupied the post once held by Wickham. "All I ask of your honor," she wrote, "is to visit this prisoner for five—nay three—minutes, in her wretchedness. And you will ask no more to convince you of the position of her claim on your humanity."

In due time, Mr. Long acknowledged her request. His brief note expressed his regrets that because of other pressing affairs, he was unable to attend to the matter she had mentioned. Mrs. Hanlon wrote him again, pleading Anne's case even more eloquently. His reply was curt, saying that it was not believable that the government, or any government, could keep a person, particularly a female, so long confined without a specific charge.

"You have done your utmost," said Anne, when Mrs. Hanlon disconsolately read her this last missive. "No one can do more."

But the woman, who had once seemed afraid of her own shadow, only looked the more determined. "I shall write him again and again. I shall make him pay attention."

It was now October. In county Wicklow the hillside was a riot of color. It was a time of village festivals, when neighbors met at each farm in turn to gather the harvest and to sing and dance until dawn. For Anne, it meant only that her fourth prison winter was on its way.

Pain was her constant companion these days, too faithful to leave her a moment's peace. She was always feverish, sometimes delirious.

In her hallucinations her dark closet became peopled with a stream of visitors: Timothy Campbell, the Heppenstall's first butler, whom she had taken for a frivolous man but who had turned out to be a patriot; Terry Byrne, his hands behind his back, going serenely to the scaffold and taking with him a piece of her heart; Michael Dwyer and her other cousins at their country "seat" in the Vale of

Imaal; Robert Emmet in the prison yard, ball and racket in hand, saying, "Anne, dear, I want you to tell everything you know about me."

Then all those whom she had loved in different ways would retreat to give way for others: the ugly, gnarled Tom Halpin, who had sold his soul for a high position; Major Sirr, the bombastic, brutal chief of police; the former Castle secretaries, Marsden and Wickham, suave and polished Englishmen who had used all their skills to get a servant girl to betray her own; Dr. Trevor with his hypocritical handsome face. They were all standing over her, shouting and pointing at her:

"Give us the names of Mr. Ellis' visitors." "Tell us where the conspirators are." "You do not want to be responsible for any harm to your aged parents or your sick little brother, do you, Anne?" "You are a most incorrigible girl, dead to all the kindness and noble feelings that adorn the character of a woman." "You are going to be hanged, Anne Devlin, and that within five days."

"Dear God, make them leave me alone," she screamed out.

Joan of Arc rode by in her shining armor and on her white steed. "Ah, Joan, you died but once and then it was over. Myself, I've died a thousand times." And then she wept.

Her father, his beard as black as in his youth, walked in and sat cross-legged at the side of her pallet. "When I was a prisoner at Wicklow gaol, Anne, I heard a prophecy. They say that one day a giant with red hair and two thumbs on each hand will spring full-grown to set Ireland free from invaders. . . ."

Her fancies died away and real voices came to replace them.

"And where is she, madam, this female prisoner about whom you have already delivered to me a mountain of correspondence?" The speaker had a haughty, cultivated, English-accented voice.

"She is here, your Honor, I will say no more. You can see for yourself."

Her door opened. Anne saw a stranger silhouetted against the hall light—an elegant gentleman in a long greatcoat, his wig carefully curled and fastened in a queue. She heard him gasp as the foul air of her close abode reached his nostrils, and he raised a white handkerchief to his face.

"Come, come, madam," he said quickly. "Follow me."

Without another glance in Anne's direction, he turned and left, Mrs. Hanlon with him.

She knew without being told that the visitor was Secretary Long, to whom her persistent friend had never given up writing. With his disappearance she felt her last thin fragments of hope go glimmering. But only a few moments later, the tower keeper's widow returned, reopening her door wide. Her face was radiant.

"Anne, darling Anne, you are free!" she cried out jubilantly. "This is the happiest day of my life. Now you can go home."

18

The Reunion

"I would take you home, Anne, but I cannot bear witnessing the scene of your restoration to your relatives. You will forgive me. Tell them I will come to you in a few days."

Mrs. Hanlon leaned into the coach and pressed Anne's hand, then turned rapidly and walked away, finding any further farewell beyond her strength. The coachman whipped up his horses, and for the last time Anne drove through the great gate of Dublin Castle. It was evening. The city was quiet, and dark except for the infrequent flares of the street lanterns. At Anne's side were Mrs. Hanlon's sister and brother-in-law, recruited to escort her to her family. They had wrapped a blanket around her, though it was not cold, and they were pleasantly solicitous of her welfare, urging the coachman to proceed gently, and asking Anne over and over whether the damp night air affected her adversely, or if the jolting over the cobblestones caused her discomfort.

Unreal! She was having another dream—like so many others. It could not be she, riding in a fine hired coach, dressed like a gentlewoman in the dark cloak and bonnet

Mrs. Hanlon had given her, her hair washed and carefully combed, and a bit of red rubbed on her lips and cheeks to disguise her prison pallor. Likely she would soon wake up and find herself in her dark closet.

"Where are we?" she asked.

"On Thomas Street," said Mrs. Hanlon's brother-in-law, whose name she had not caught. "St. Catherine's Church here to the left. 'Tis rather a landmark. A pity you cannot see it clearly." He spoke as if she were a tourist, viewing Dublin for the first time. Obviously Mrs. Hanlon had told him nothing of her history.

"Ah, yes," said Mrs. Hanlon's sister. "It was in front of this church that brave Robert Emmet was executed. Perhaps you heard about it." She, too, seemed to have the impression that Anne was a visitor from a far country. "They took his life but they gave all Ireland a hero. Those ringing words of his splendid speech at the trial have sounded around the world, translated in I don't know how many languages. Have you read it, Miss Devlin?"

"No, ma'am," Anne admitted meekly.

"William Pitt was responsible," announced her husband. "He sent his spies to France to persuade Robert Emmet and his friends that the time was ripe for a revolt. It's all come out now. Pitt wanted to be prime minister again and hoped by making trouble in Ireland he'd discredit Henry Addington, his successor. Against that wily politician, Emmet never had a chance. He and his followers were the victims of a foul intrigue."

Lucky now that it was night, so that this well-meaning couple could not see the tears streaming down her face.

"Robert Emmet and Sarah Curran," sighed the woman. "What a beautiful love story! After Robert died and her father disowned her, she went quite out of her mind. Friends in Cork took her in and nursed her back to health. I hear she's married to an English captain now. Does that mean she's forgotten her Irish rebel sweetheart?"

"How her face used to light up when she received his letters!" murmured Anne.

"What?" The woman looked at her sharply and then shook her head, deciding, no doubt, that Anne's illness was making her talk wildly.

The coach had turned left and was jogging down those same narrow, disreputable streets along which Anne had torn the day she delivered Robert Emmet's white shirt to the Thomas Street depot. At one of the wretched gabled houses whose inhabitants she had so pitied, the coachman drew his horses to a stop.

"Here we are, Miss Devlin." The man jumped down. "Take it easy now."

He and the coachman had to carry her down the dark, ill-smelling hallway and up the rotten rickety staircase. They set her down by a door on the attic floor. "I believe this is the place."

"You have been kind," said Anne, holding out her hand. "I'll wish you good night."

"You wouldn't want us to wait?'

"No." Her tone was firm. "I'll be all right now."

She leaned against the wall for support as she listened to their footsteps receding down the stairs. For the first time that day she was sure she was not dreaming. Then she knocked.

An old woman, slender and white-haired, opened the door and stared uncertainly into the shadows.

"You are looking for someone, miss?"

"Mother!" gasped Anne.

They were in each other's arms.

" 'Tis Anne! Anne is here!"

The words, incredulous and joyous, echoed around the dismal crowded room, lit with a single candle and smoke-filled from the small chimneyless stove. Briefly, it seemed to Anne that the cries of delight were uttered by a group of strangers. The two gaunt young men in tattered shirts and faded breeches who seized her by the shoulders to pull her inside—she had to look twice before she knew her brothers, John and Little Arthur. Mary and Julie—were they these two emaciated young women in patched and shabby aprons? Even as they embraced her wildly, she was aware of their too translucent skin, the artificial flush of their cheeks, advanced symptoms of that ruthless enemy, tuberculosis.

"Your father is sleeping," said her mother. "How happy he will be to wake and find you here!"

Anne tried to take a step and tottered.

"You are ill, Anne!" Julie cried with sudden awareness. "How selfish of us not to notice!"

They smothered her with exclamations of pity and compassion, as gentle hands lowered her into a chair. It was the same straw one she remembered from her childhood, an extravagance purchased from a tinker. The only souvenir of their former life, she would learn later. She sank into it gratefully.

"Should we put you to bed? Would you like to rest?"

Anne shook her head. "I've rested too long."

"We have been out of our mind," sobbed her mother, stroking her hair. "We could find out nothing about you—nothing. I went to wait on Dr. Trevor. 'Madam,' he said, 'your daughter has been transferred to Naas gaol.' In Kildare. I took a trip there . . ."

"She insisted," interposed Mary. "Julie and I—she said we could never do it, and John and Little Arthur could not leave their work—or we would starve. She walked—asking for food along the way like a beggar . . ." The indignation that this should have happened to her beloved parent exploded like a rocket.

"It was not too hard," resumed Mrs. Devlin. "I would not have minded if I could have seen you, even for five minutes. They had never heard of you at Naas. I made my way back and went again to Dr. Trevor. 'You were cruel to let me go to Naas to seek my daughter,' I told him. He pretended regret. 'I pledge you my honor, madam,' he said. 'I do not know where she can be.' That was all I could get out of him."

"I was in the tower of the Castle," Anne explained. "On Trevor's orders."

"We knew he was a liar!" exclaimed Little Arthur. "Ah, the blackguard." He clenched his fists.

"Let the Lord punish him in His own way," remonstrated their mother, without malice.

"I would like to see him," Anne cried out exultantly, her eyes shining. "I would like to tell him that now I am free—free as he is. And that I can hold my head high—as he cannot."

"What is going on here? What is the disturbance?" From a mattress in the corner, an old man with thin white hair and beard raised himself on his elbow. "Who is she?" He pointed at Anne with a trembling finger.

"Father!" Anne burst out. "Ah, but I am glad to see you!" He only looked blank.

"Father, it is I! Anne!"

"Anne," he repeated dully. "I had a daughter named Anne once. A little thing with curly hair and laughter bubbling from her like water from a spring in Imaal." He fell back on the mattress and closed his eyes, muttering incoherently.

Anne looked from one member of her family to another, bewildered.

"You should know, Anne." John rested his hand on her shoulder. "Father's mind is sometimes clouded. It is not surprising after what they did to him."

That her own father should not know her! Anne winced with horror. She should have realized that her long dreamed-of homecoming would be fraught with sorrow beyond bearing. Only her wish not to hurt them kept her from crying aloud at the cruelty of fate.

Her mother sensed her mood. "You are in time for supper, Anne," she said brightly and bravely. "Tonight it will be a celebration such as we have never known. To have my children with me again, that was all I ever asked." She rose. "Julie, will you help me serve?"

Supper was dry bread and a thin and tasteless gruel ladled out in wooden bowls. The family pulled up straw mattresses and sat around Anne, as they ate. Furniture was as scarce in their humble abode as at Butterfield Lane, but they were together—that was all that mattered. Everything else was unimportant, even the physical pain that racked her body.

The first shock at the sad state to which her family had been reduced soon vanished. She was with those whom she loved and who loved her. Companionship—was there anything in the world more beautiful? Conversation flowed, slowly and awkwardly at first, and then in torrents, the warmth of it better than wine or fire. In this warmth, all their terrible experiences were transmuted to tales told around a hearthside—tales of a past that had really nothing to do with them.

"The day after our arrest," said John, "they took me away to the Ship Street guardhouse. For more than twenty-four hours I had nothing to eat or drink. Then a woman who had brought some tea for her husband took pity on me and offered me a cup. I was raising it to my lips, when the guard spied me and shattered it with his bayonet."

With all John had endured, he was still the luckiest. A gentleman of high rank, who was at the guardhouse in search of one of his workmen, had been impressed with his youthful appearance and frank manner and had personally arranged for his release. His imprisonment had lasted only a few weeks.

Little Arthur had had no such good fortune. Because of his name, he had been mistaken for the "wanted criminal," their cousin, Big Art. To make him "confess," he had been strung up on the triangle and flogged unmercifully. He raised his shirt to show Anne the long, ugly welts across his back.

"The brutes!" she cried out forgetting her own long sufferings.

"I did not make a sound," he confided proudly. "Every time the whip struck, I told myself that one new patriot was being born in Ireland." But it had been months before the festering wounds had begun to heal, and even now, three years later, the least exertion renewed the old throbbing.

"You will want to know about Nellie," said their mother.

"Yes," Anne breathed. The last she had heard—from little Jimmy—was that her baby sister could not be found. She had hardly dared to ask about her, fearing bad news.

"She is fine." Mrs. Devlin smiled wistfully. "The welfare agent learned that a farmer and his wife had taken her in. A worthy, God-fearing couple. On my way to Kildare I passed by the place. I saw her in the garden, pretty and healthy, playing merrily with her new brothers and sisters. I did not stop. 'Twas better thus. How could I bring her here, with Death hovering so near, deciding which of us he should choose first? Now she will have a chance at the happiness which we cannot give her . . ." Her voice trailed off.

"Do you remember the schoolmaster, Anne?" demanded Little Arthur. "The day we came home from gathering turf in the bog. How comical he looked, flopping along like a scarecrow! And how noble his soul! 'Long live Homer!' he cried and bowed farewell to all of us, even Miss Melinda." He chuckled, and then broke off—coughing.

"I remember," said Anne softly. " 'May we meet again when Ireland is free,' he told us. He was that sure our day would come."

There was a stirring from the mattress in the corner. Her father was pulling himself to his feet. John and Little Arthur rushed to help him.

"What's going on here? What's the disturbance?" His gaze rested on Anne. A first look of doubt was rapidly replaced by one of overwhelming satisfaction. "Daughter! So you've come home at last." Supported by his sons, he moved toward her with the halting steps of the aged, but his eyes were clear and his voice was firm. "I always knew you were too much of a Devlin to let iron bars and stone walls stop you from where you wanted to go!"

Then they were all laughing and sobbing until Anne felt her heart would burst.

Post Note

Health returned to Anne Devlin slowly after her release from prison. In time she married "an industrious and upright man named Campbell"—there is no record of his first name. They had two children, a boy and a girl. She lived in obscurity and died in poverty on September 18, 1851, at the age of seventy. Only after her death was there widespread recognition of her heroic role in Ireland's long struggle for freedom. Beneath the Celtic Cross which marks her grave at Glasnevin Cemetery is the inscription: "To the Memory of ANNE DEVLIN—The Faithful Servant of Robert Emmet, who possessed some rare and many noble qualities."

Printed in Great Britain by
Lowe and Brydone (Printers) Limited, London, N.W.10